An Inn Decent
Proposal

By
Sharon Buchbinder

**Book Design & Formatting:
Wicked Muse**

**Cover Art Provided By:
Rae Monet**

Sharon Buchbinder

Who Let the Jinni Out of the Bottle...

SharonBuchbinder.com

www.sharonbuchbinder.com

An Inn Decent Proposal

TABLE OF CONTENTS

DEDICATION

To my husband, Dale, who has filled my life with love and romance for over 40 years; to all the great chefs and hoteliers, whose gifts make our taste buds dance and our bodies sigh with the pleasure of a good bed and the comforts of home.

AN INN DECENT PROPOSAL

"But you wanted the Inn, didn't you?"

Genie placed a tentative hand on his.

"Yes—but what I did was *crazy*." Jim shook his head. "I spent every dime I had, plus every one *you* had. Now what do we do?"

She let out a long breath. "We do what we're good at. I'm an outstanding chef. You're an experienced hotel manager. We're under forty. We have our health and are *extremely* motivated to succeed. I'd say we have an embarrassment of riches. Partners?" She extended a hand.

A small flame of hope flickered in Jim's mind. He reached out and squeezed her fingers. "Seriously?"

"Yes." She withdrew her hand slowly and sipped her latte. "Why did you want *this* place?"

"The old girl called to me, begged me to save her." He gave Genie a wistful smile. "Do I sound crazy?"

"You call the Inn 'she,' too?"

"Yes, she's like a grand old dame who's fallen on hard times. Remember the parties? The famous people who stayed and played there? Celebrities came to the Inn because they knew their privacy and secrets were safe with us. If those walls could talk! Every day was new and exciting. I would love to bring back her glory days."

Genie leaped up, ran around the table, and threw her arms around him. "I have the same dream. We *can* do it."

Jim hesitated for a moment, then returned the gesture, his hands unable to resist lingering on her luscious curves just a tad too long. Genie's inviting cleavage made him wish they were somewhere private. He could scarcely breathe and had to shake his head to dispel naughty images of nuzzling her soft breasts. "We can do what?"

CHAPTER ONE

Jim Rawlings pulled his car into a parking space on the shady street in front of the Victory Shores Inn and gazed at the huge real estate sign posted on the rusted iron fence.

Public Auction 10 AM
July 3rd

How appropriate the old gal would go up on the block today. She'd hosted some pretty terrific Independence Day parties back in the day, complete with fireworks on the lake. For over a century, the Victory Shores Inn had bustled with life and vigor, a vacation destination for the rich, famous, and wannabe famous. Now she looked like a decrepit old crone, suitable only for haunting or for starring in the latest in teenage slasher flicks.

He drummed his fingers on the steering wheel, his mind clicking through the odds for getting her up and running.

In the plus column, he had a degree from Cornell's School of Hotel Administration and knew the hospitality business inside and out. Jim knew everything from the basement up to the attic in the care and feeding of a hotel and its guests. During his education, he had learned the business of managing a hotel from grounds keeping up to marketing and profit margins. His internship and employment experiences provided the nitty-gritty of the real world. He had unblocked toilets, repaired leaking pipes, managed angry housekeeping staff, and worked through hurricanes, blizzards, and floods. Hotel management was a twenty-four hours a day, seven days a week business and he loved it. Best part of all, being busy kept his mind off his obsession—gambling.

On the minus side of the equation, renovations wouldn't be cheap and repairs—most of which he planned to do himself—would take time. And, there was one more detail he needed to nail down after he bought the place. He had to find an outstanding executive chef. Not just any toque-topped slice-and-dice genius would do for this Inn.

No, he wanted, and the old gal deserved, a world-class *chef de cuisine* on a par with those found in the Big Apple, Vegas—or La Bonne Chance Resort and Casino. No matter how beautiful the setting, the service and fine dining *always* drove the bottom line. Great chefs were not easy to find, nor were they cheap. Maybe a new Culinary Institute of America graduate would be interested in getting in on the ground floor and having his or her own kitchen? After a year or two, the chef might move on to a larger or more opulent venue, but that was a chance he'd have to take. Tomorrow, after the deal was inked, he'd call the CIA and other culinary schools to see if they could recommend an up and coming *hungry* new graduate.

Couples cruised the tree-lined streets, some with luxurious baby strollers, the kind that practically drove itself and brewed a latte for you. He tried to recall the last time he'd been back in Victory Shores. Had it really been fifteen years? He let out a low whistle and shook his head. Almost two decades and the town seemed like it was trapped in a time warp. As far as he could tell, very little had changed—well, except for the pitiful husk of a hotel in front of him.

Lucky for him, the teachers had all liked him back then. Otherwise, he'd still be the oldest senior in Victory Shores High School. He rubbed the medallion in his pocket, a gift from a good friend, and winced as memories floated back, reminding him of his many screw-ups. It wasn't as if he was stupid. Hell, he'd had nearly perfect scores on his SAT exams. But homework and classes took a backseat to more pressing matters of poker and ponies. Men with heavy accents had phoned his parents' house day and night, issuing thinly veiled threats about Jim and the money he owed their *associates*.

Over and over, his mom and dad begged him to stop, alternating between threats, tears, and self-recriminations. They didn't cause his addiction to gambling, they couldn't control it, nor could they cure it. When he learned his parents had put a second mortgage on their house to keep him safe, guilt and remorse overwhelmed him. He left town for good the night of his graduation from Victory Shores High School, telling his teary-eyed mom and red-faced dad that he'd be back once he'd made a name for himself. That day had arrived at last, but his folks were gone, taken in a head-on collision with a drunk driver three weeks after he left town.

He climbed out of the car, opened the shrieking gate, and plucked an empty cigarette pack from the overgrown weeds covering what had once been a beautiful plant-lined walkway. At the older and wiser age of thirty-seven, he wished he could travel back in time and smack some sense into his eighteen-year-old self. *What was I thinking?* He had hopped from casino to casino, eking out a living as a waiter to support his mounting habit—until he hit his own personal rock bottom. And the rocks didn't get much harder. To this day, he could still smell the stink of an Atlantic City low tide as it washed over his nearly unconscious body while thugs in steel-toed boots tuned him up for not paying back his bookie in a timely manner.

Had it not been for the sudden appearance of an amorous couple under the boardwalk, he wouldn't be alive today. Later he learned the man who saved his life was in town for the Atlantic City Professional Body Building contest—and pissed as hell that he only came in third. Jim rubbed the scar on his eyebrow and mentally thanked the man who came in first that day. From what he heard, the thugs hadn't expected the muscle man be able to get out of his own way, much less beat the snot out of both of them.

Apparently, the hoods had never heard of a body-builder with a black sash in Kung Fu. A concussion, a broken jaw, fifty stitches, and a nearly ripped off ear had taught Jim the consequences of his poor choices. When he was discharged from the hospital, the first thing he did was find a Gamblers Anonymous meeting. Ninety meetings in ninety days, a sponsor, and working the twelve-step program delivered him into recovery—but he knew he could not be "cured." Years later, he attended at least one meeting a week, sometimes more and never felt it was a waste of time—especially when he was able to help a newcomer who was certain he could "quit whenever he or she wanted to."

He might be back where he started, but this time he was clear eyed and driven by a will to succeed, rather than the thrill of a wager. He turned and eyed the object of his affection. The Victory Shores Inn, once a gorgeous centerpiece of the little town, had fallen on tough times.

Although overgrown with ivy, the two-story white Federalist-style building with the colonnaded guest wing to the right of the main entrance still enjoyed a charisma that hadn't faded despite its age and disrepair. He climbed the flaking brick steps, avoiding broken rocking chairs, crumbling concrete, and the debris of days gone by.

Leaning on what appeared to be a solid column, Jim closed his eyes and recalled serving drinks and hor d'oeurves to well-dressed, well-heeled guests at this very spot. He'd been brazen, telling them he was saving money for college. Little did the heavy tippers know, they were supporting his shameful habit, not his quest for higher education. He turned and patted the old gal's wall. Large chunks of peeling paint on the trim revealed pockmarks and pits beneath. Damage from freezing winters and sizzling summers. He sighed. She needed a *lot* of work.

There were no twelve-step programs for run down hotels—but Jim had enough Gamblers Anonymous experience to share with everyone, including this dame. He'd done his homework, gotten an in-depth inspection report. Down, but not out, it was time to get her back on her feet. If he could do it for himself, he knew he could do it for her.

He crunched through weeds and kicked empty beer cans to the side on his way back to his car. The bank was still open. He'd bring a cashier's check for the largest amount of money he'd ever been able to save in his life—half a million dollars. He touched the medallion once more for good luck.

By noon tomorrow, the Victory Shores Inn would be his. No one in their right mind would out-bid him. One thing Jim understood was odds, and the odds of that happening were a million to one—of *that,* Jim was one hundred percent certain.

Genie King sat at her chipped Formica kitchen counter and ran her index finger down the spreadsheet for the fourth time in the last thirty minutes. The reserve price for the auction was two hundred and fifty thousand dollars. Knowing Beth Head, Genie was certain the realtor's obnoxious husband, Richard, aka, Dick Head, would be there as a plant in the audience to bid up the price. If she bought the Victory Shores Inn for three hundred thousand that would leave her another two hundred thousand to fix it up. But if she had to go as high as four hundred, that meant she'd have to obtain a home equity line on top of the mortgage she'd already taken out on her home.

She'd done her homework. She knew *all* about the cosmetic and structural issues, having already invested five hundred dollars for a top to bottom inspection. The twenty-three page report, complete with color photos and recommended repairs had been brutally honest. The good news was the ten year old roof was still in good shape, and the foundation remained sound. *Thank God.* However, everything in between and surrounding the Inn was a different story. From peeling paint and rotting interior wood floors to overgrown gardens, the old gal was going to require a major labor of love. And be an enormous headache.

The local community college had a horticulture and landscape design program. As soon as Genie sealed the deal, she'd call the program director to ask about interns. Heck, they could do an entire course around the Inn! All the maintenance men she knew from work had side hustles on top of their full time jobs, so she felt pretty sure she could get them to help her with repairs at a reasonable price. She knew it would be a challenge and a lot of work. While she might not be a lawyer, she knew what questions to ask, how to read a contract, and how *not* to be conned by a dishonest contractor.

Genie sighed and imagined herself sipping a mint julep on the shaded colonnaded guest wing porch, one of her favorite features of the Inn. She had fallen head over heels for the place the first day she sat in the job interview with the owner way back in her freshman year of high school. She'd been what? Fourteen?

The owner had inspected her working papers, reminded her she could only work after school and on weekends while classes were in session, but that in the summer, she could rely on full time employment. At the end of the meeting, her new boss had told her that she had a good feeling about Genie and her future in the hospitality industry. Little did her supervisor know that one day the young girl in front of her would come back to claim the Inn as her own. She smiled at the thought—then gnawed at her bottom lip when the butterflies of worry crowded out those of excitement.

If *only* Mom and Dad were still alive. Five years had passed, but she missed both of them every single day. Mom had taken care of everyone; so much so, that she never took care of herself. When she found out she had uterine cancer, the disease had spread so far and so fast, she survived only six months. Dad died six months later of a broken heart. They left everything to Genie, including the home she still lived in, free and clear of debts. She wiped a tear off her cheek. She could really use their advice, financial or otherwise.

Always supportive, Mom would have asked, "Will it make you happy? Will you have time for yourself? Will you have a social life?"

Always practical and cautious, Dad would have asked, "Do you have business plan? A mission statement? An exit strategy if it doesn't work out?"

Would it make her happy? Would she have time for herself? Would she have a social life? Right now, she was miserable, had no time for herself, and her social life was nonexistent. Nuns got more action. Genie didn't even have a potted plant, for fear it would die of neglect. Her life revolved around preparing and presenting food and— much to her chagrin—her waistline showed it. Tasting went along with cooking. How could *anyone* trust a skinny chef?

Her education from the world's premier

culinary college culminated in a Bachelor's of Professional Studies in Culinary Arts. A Culinary Institute of America, or CIA, graduate was *always* looking for an opportunity to be the head chef. The towns surrounding the school were bursting at the seams with bistros, cafes, brasseries, and pubs run by CIA trained graduates. Genie aspired to do more with her knowledge, skills, and attitude. Her goal on graduation was to apprentice with a James Beard Award winning establishment to become an even better restauranteur.

The saying, "Be careful what you wish for—it might come true!" flitted through her mind as she absentmindedly folded up her paperwork. She recalled how flattered and excited she had been to be recruited by one of the highest end restaurants in the East, Asiatique, the premiere French fusion restaurant of La Bonne Chance Resort and Casino. This was the opportunity she'd been dreaming of for years.

Genie had leaped at the chance to learn from Jean-François Boyer, one of the top executive chefs in the country. Handsome, talented, fluent in seven languages, Jean-François swaggered his way into her heart. A year into the job and the relationship, however, she discovered she was not the only woman who warmed the cockles of his heart—and his bed. When confronted, he laughed at her and told her she should be grateful, few men wanted a fat woman. Besides, she wasn't that good in bed *or* the kitchen. She was lucky to work for him.

She didn't know which stung worse—the fat comment or the insults to her cooking abilities. Genie wasn't just a good sous chef, she was the *de facto* exécutive chef who ensured the quality of every dish that left the kitchen. Without her working eighteen hours a day, seven days a week, the meals in that sweat shop would be overdone, underdone, unflavored, flaccid—or toxic.

Behind his back, the staff called him Chef Boyer-Dee, because his most famous and only dish he personally oversaw was one that suited his fiery temperament, Shrimp Fra Diavolo. Every employee down to the busboys, dishwashers, and cleaning people feared and hated him and his volcanic temper.

After that confrontation, not only did she refuse to go to bed with him, she began looking for other jobs. She sent out her resume and was rejected repeatedly, even by former classmates. When questioned about why her application was dismissed, one woman with a niche restaurant in Red Hook, confessed she'd gotten a call from Genie's boss, screaming, "How dare you try to steal my sous chef! I'll ruin you!" Each time she attempted to apply for another job, his snitches in the industry alerted him. Over time, the explosions had become predictable. She would apply for a new job.

A few days later, he would emerge from his office, apoplectic, black eyes bulging, veins standing out on his bull neck. The other employees would vanish like a flock of sparrows when a hawk flew down and snatched one of their own. Alone and unarmed save for her self-esteem and steel spine, she would face the screaming black haired madman. He would begin in profanity laced French, which thanks to her years in high school language classes with headphones and recorded conversations, she understood with crystal clarity.

Transitioning to English, he would give her a tongue lashing that included his favorite words, "ingrate" "incompetent," and "inept." During his last outburst, Chef Boyer-Dee escalated from verbal to physical abuse and threw a large iron skillet at her. She'd dodged it, picked it up, and thrown it back at him. The astonished look on the lunatic's face and silence were worth the risk. The dent in the wall, however, was evidence enough that it was time to leave before she lost her mind *and* her self-esteem. Short of leaving New York State, the only place she'd ever called home, her only way out was to own her own business.

Exit plan from her new exit plan? Worst-case scenario, she'd fail, go bankrupt, be forced to return to some other executive chef's kitchen as a sous chef. Her stomach knotted at the thought of working for yet another temperamental *bête noir*. What she *really* needed to find was someone with hotel management expertise. With Cornell's School of Hotel Administration in geographic striking distance, she anticipated she could find a hungry young man or woman willing to start on the ground floor of the historic Inn's renaissance.

Once she had the title to the property in her hand, she'd make a call to the career center and post a job description. She *had* to make this work. If she couldn't make a go of it with the Inn, she'd lose everything—lock, stock, and cooking pot.

The living room clock cuckooed eight times and her heart stuttered. Almost time to go and she wasn't even dressed. Good thing she'd selected her outfit for the auction the night before. She dashed to the bathroom and showered quickly.

Genie swiped the towel across the steam fogged mirror and revealed a face surrounded by long ringlets of copper colored hair. She aimed the hairdryer at the remaining mist and worked at pulling her unruly curls back in a ponytail. Or should she wear it down? After all, it was an auction, not a kitchen. There was no hazard of hair falling in the food. *What the heck.* It was a day for taking chances.

She let her hair down, and went to work on her makeup. The woman at the cosmetic counter had assured her the color palette in her hand complemented her blue eyes and freckled complexion. At this moment in time, Genie wasn't sure the bronze and blue shades were right, but she plunged on feeling daring and somewhat dangerous. The hardest part was yet to come.

Her new black suit and cobalt blue blouse awaited her in the closet. She'd been dieting, trying to lose the pesky fifteen pounds that followed her around like a faithful dog. The moment of truth was at hand. She took a deep breath and put on the blouse. *Holy crap.* How had she not noticed the low-cut neckline before today? Had the saleslady been holding the blouse up when she looked in the mirror? The skirt was a tad tighter than she had hoped it would be. *Dammit.* Well, at least it zipped. She put on the jacket and faced the mirror.

Great Caesar's ghost! *Sweet Charity* meets *Nine to Five.* She looked like a ginger haired stand in for Dolly Parton. The clock cuckooed nine. She slammed the closet door, stomped into the living room, and glared at the annoying timepiece. "Shut up, you stupid bird!" *Maybe it's time to rip the cuckoo out of the clock.*

Mortified that she would even *think* of destroying a memento her father gave her mother more than three decades ago, she whispered, "Sorry. I didn't really mean it. I'm just nervous." She thought she saw a glint in the old bird's eyes, but no, it was the tears in hers.

Time to go. Though she wasn't Roman Catholic, she didn't want to take any chances today, of all days, and said a quick prayer to Saint Lawrence, the patron saint of chefs. Couldn't hurt, right? She stopped mid-jog to the front door. Maybe Saint Rita, the patron saint of impossible dreams would be a better choice.

On the other hand, why not pray to Saint Cayetano? After all, wasn't she just about to take the biggest risk in her entire thirty-three years of life? Surely, the patron saint of gamblers would turn the odds in her favor to get the winning bid—hopefully with money to spare.

CHAPTER TWO

Beth Head paced the gloomy foyer of the Victory Shores Inn and for the tenth time that morning rearranged the brochures on the registration desk. It might help if she could get more light in the room. She toggled the light switches to no avail and threw the front door open to allow the sun and heat into the oppressive space.

Pausing to admire her reflection in the ceiling to floor mirror at the entrance, she fluffed her short blonde hair, and touched up her blood red lipstick. After a quick glance out the door to be sure she was alone, Beth reached into her bra and lifted her breasts for better display. She could have bought a friggin' townhouse with the money she spent on plastic surgery. For the price she paid, these girls deserved to be up and out on a silver platter.

Where the hell is Dick? He'd better not stand her up today. She needed him there to jack up the crowd into a bidding war. Not that *she* wanted the dreary dump. She shuddered at the thought. Reeking of old cigars and older dust and mildew, the place gave her the creeps and made her itch. She was breaking out in hives just being here. What if it was mold? That could screw the sale up royally. She hoped no one thought to look for that. No, she'd be sure to emphasize, this is an *as is* sale, folks. Take it or leave it. *Dammit.* A car door slammed shut.

"Well, about time you got here," she called.

The man who stomped into the front door wasn't Dick—in fact, she wasn't sure he was even human. Short, dark, and hirsute with knuckles practically scraping the ground, the Neanderthal walked into her personal space and exhaled garlic into her face. No, he could *not* seriously be thinking about buying the Inn. He *had* to be lost, in search of a bar—or the Victory Zoo. He would scare away the real bidders. She had to get rid of him. She took a deep breath and gave her best sales person welcome. "Are you lost?"

Ending with a popping sound, he said "Nope" and exhaled more pungent aromas her way.

Please, please, please don't be here for the auction. "I'm Beth Head. What can I do to help you?"

He glanced around the room, ignoring her extended hand. "I'm here to buy dis place."

"Pardon me?"

"Dis here is an auction, right?"

"Well, um, yes, yes it is," she stammered. *Ohmygawd. This gorilla is a buyer?* She snapped out of her stupor and into sales mode. "Please take this brochure and feel free to wander around. The Victory Shores Inn is over a hundred years old and has a great history. F. Scott Fitzgerald and his wife, Zelda, summered here—"

"Zip it."

"Pardon me?" As a warm flush ran up her neck and face, her *sang froid* melted and threatened to reach the boiling point.

"I don't give a shit 'bout no Xena. When I want you to talk, I'll rattle your cage."

Suppressing the urge to tell the

Neanderthal off, Beth's mouth snapped shut. *Where was Dick?* If she ever needed the Victory Shores Chief of Police at her side, *this* was the freaking day.

As if on cue, Dick's voice boomed into the foyer. "Honey, I'm home." He bounded in the front door, dressed in a custom suit looking more like he was about to go to work on Wall Street, not on the Victory Shores Police Department, or VSPD. "Ah, Tony, I see you found the place." He clapped the stocky man on the back. "Take a tour, it's gonna be all yours soon."

Tony's close-set eyes darted around the foyer and sitting area. "Dis place come wid a terlet?"

It took a moment for Beth to translate his request. "Yes, the men's room is down the hall, on the left." Good thing she'd brought toilet paper, hand soap, and guest towels. She hoped he used them.

As Tony shambled away, Beth grabbed her husband's arm and hissed at him. "Dis? Dem? Terlet? What kind of beast *is* he? And how do *you* know him?"

"Hey, you know what they say about

judging a book by its cover," Dick chided. "Tony Aiolfo's got a lot of loot. After he sets up shop here, he'll be making generous donations to our favorite charity—us."

Horrified at the possibilities, she demanded, "And what *exactly* do you do in return for your new found furry friend?"

Dick glanced around, then gave her a wink. "VSPD will give him, shall we say, certain considerations."

"And what *is* his business?"

"This and that."

"You have reached a new low—which I didn't think was possible." Dizzy with rage, Beth could barely speak. "My realtor's license is *not* going on the line for your latest scam. Everything that happens today goes *by the book*."

"Beth, c'mon, you gotta work with me," Dick wheedled.

Just then, car doors slammed shut and a man's voice called out, "Hello? Anyone here?"

A throaty woman's voice responded. "I think we need to go inside. I doubt they'll have the auction out here."

Footsteps clomped up the stairs. A Nicholas Cage look-alike entered first, blinking rapidly to adjust to the gloom.

Well hello, handsome. Beth shot a glance at her buffoon of a husband, now deep in a huddle with the returned gorilla, and made a quick comparison. Dick came up far short.

Her attention shifted to the sound of high heels clicking on the hardwood floor. The woman who came in behind the hunk looked as if she belonged in an executive bordello. With bright red hair cascading over both shoulders and a low-cut blouse that exposed ample cleavage that exceeded Beth's own store bought bust, it took her a full minute to realize who the curvaceous sexpot was.

"Genie King? Is that really you?" Beth adjusted the girls before bounding over to give the other woman an embrace and air kisses. "It's been years! I almost didn't recognize you out of your maid's uniform."

Genie extracted herself from Beth's hug, face flushed and a frown creasing her brow. "I ended my career here as a prep cook, remember? You used to tell your all friends to steer clear of the red head with the butcher knife—"

Faux smile plastered to her face, Beth pivoted away from the short, annoying trip down memory lane and extended a hand to the handsome man. She gave him a once over. "Beth Head, Head Realty. And you are?"

The man's slow sexy smile had Beth's neglected nether regions tingling. *Hubba, hubba. When is Dick's next business trip?*

"Jim Rawlings." He quirked an eyebrow, making him even more attractive, if that was possible. "I see you haven't changed a bit, Beth."

"Ohmygawd! It's been so long. What have you been up to?"

To her supreme annoyance, he ignored Beth and turned to Genie. "You seem familiar—but I can't place you. Should I know you?"

Heat crawled up Genie's skin from her breasts to her neck and face. *Should he know me?* At the time they'd been working together— every summer from middle school through high school— she had known everything about Jim Rawlings—where he lived, what car he drove, how many poker games he played a week—to name but a few of his favorite things. Jim had been four years ahead of her in school—although everyone knew he wasn't very attentive to his studies back in the day. Today people would say she was *obsessed* with him, verging on the substance of a restraining order. Seventeen years ago, before stalker laws, it was simply called a major crush.

Her normally throaty voice came out in a tremulous squeak. "You and I worked together here at the Inn. Every summer."

"Skinny little Genie?" Jim stepped back, gave her a long head to toe look and whistled. "You filled out in all the *right* places."

Warmth flushed Genie's cheeks again. He *liked* her curves? *Really?*

Flustered by his intense stare, Genie groped for an intelligent thought—and grasped at the first thing that came to mind. "Beth, do we have time to look around one more time before the auction begins?"

The realtor pursed her crimson lips and frowned. "Yes, just be back in fifteen minutes. We start *exactly* at ten."

Beth had been in the popular clique in high school. She'd never missed an opportunity to make snide comments to her buddies about those who worked at the Inn, as opposed to partying at it. The tables were turned, it seemed. Beth was now forced to suck up to the high school outcast. *Karma.* Shaking her head, Genie reminded herself today was the day to place Beth's condescending digs where they belonged—in the distant past. Pulling a notepad out as she walked, Genie made a beeline to the kitchen.

"Hold up," Jim called. "I'll go with you."

As she opened the door of the large gas range, she glanced at the tall man beside her. A touch of gray at his temples, a scar across his eyebrow and a few laugh lines around his eyes, but other than that he *still* looked good enough to eat. Urging her inner chef to simmer down, she took a deep breath. "The years have been good to you. What brings you back to Victory Shores?"

"Long story short, after leaving here, I

worked my way across the country, going from hotel to hotel. I did everything from cleaning toilets to carting luggage to rooms. Found I had a talent for taking run down properties and building them up. Decided to go back to school part time and earned a degree in hospitality from Cornell's Hotel School. Wound up working for major hotel corporations from New York City to Las Vegas. The money's okay, but when you break it down by the hours, it's probably ten bucks an hour and I'm working for someone else. I wanted my own place. And I missed small towns. How about you?"

Momentarily distracted by the ancient behemoth of a refrigerator and its internal odors, she turned and focused on Jim's question. "I'm a graduate of the CIA. I've worked with some top chefs but I want my own kitchen. Now I'm at the Asiatique at La Bonne Chance Resort and Casino."

Jim's eyebrows flew up. "Seriously?"

Miffed, she huffed, "Is that so hard to believe?"

"No, I just meant I work there, too. In the accounting department. What are the chances of my never seeing you before today?"

"Pretty good, actually. I'm in the kitchen a minimum of twelve hours a day, I'm kind of like a vampire, I guess. I don't see the sunlight—or the other floors of La Bonne Chance. I clock in, I cook, I clock out. Next day, I clock in, I cook, I try to avoid an arrogant ass of an executive chef, and I clock out."

He grinned and her knees wobbled. "Confidentially, I never set foot in Asiatique. Not in my budget."

The short, hairy guy stomped into the kitchen. "Hey, youse two love boids, I hate to interrupt dis Hallmark moment, but I'm here to buy dis here place, not go to a wedding. You guys comin' to dis auction, or not?"

Genie flushed, snapped her notebook shut and followed the troll out of the kitchen into the foyer.

Jim linked his arm through hers, pulled her close and whispered, "May the best offer win."

Best offer? She had an offer for Jim, one her girly bits thoroughly approved of by throwing a little party in her pants. Mentally groaning, she shook her head to throw off the hormone laced cloud of lust and disentangled their limbs.

"No fair." She laughed. "I need my hands free to outbid you."

The short ugly man glanced over his shoulder and snorted. "Dream on, ya dumb broad. Dis place is mine."

Her face flushed and her ears rang as if a gun had gone off. Bad enough she was abused at work. No way was she letting this knuckle-dragger get away with speaking to her in that manner. She opened her mouth to take him down a peg, but before she could say anything, Jim stepped in front of the man.

"What did you say?" Towering over the gnome by a good foot, Jim refused to let the man pass him.

"I said, dis place is mine."

In a nails-on-chalkboard falsetto, Beth called from the doorway, "I see Mr. Aiolfo found you."

All heads swiveled toward the realtor, including the ogre.

Genie swore if looks could have killed, the realtor *and* Jim would have turned the man to stone.

Beth's voice dropped an octave. "It's ten o'clock, which means it's time to begin the auction. This is my husband, Dick Head, Chief of Victory Shores Police. He's here to serve as a witness to the proceedings. Genie King, Jim Rawlings, and Tony Aiolfo are here to bid on the property known as Victory Shores Inn." Beth took a deep breath and launched into a brisk review, "Some ground rules: the *reserve* price is two hundred and fifty thousand dollars; bidding *must* be in increments of ten thousand. You *must* have sufficient cash or a cashier's check for a deposit—or the entire amount. *Everything* is due in thirty days. And, the property is sold *as is, absolutely no guarantees*. Got it?"

Dick grinned at his wife and gave her the thumbs up sign. "Let the games begin."

"What do I have for an opening bid?"

"Two-hunnert-fifty thou." Tony dug a finger in his ear and pulled out a chunk of earwax.

Genie suppressed a gag and shouted, "Three-hundred thousand."

"Tree-fifty." Tony winked at Dick. "I got

a good feeling about dis. Gonna have me a great casino."

Jim stared at Tony. "A casino? There's one not far from here in Victory. With nine-hundred rooms, twenty restaurants, not including the buffets, *and* a shopping mall, La Bonne Chance is enormous and wildly successful. It will eat you alive. Besides, this place is a historic treasure, not a slot machine parlor. I bid three-sixty."

Tony smirked, stuffed three sticks of gum into his mouth, and dropped the wrappers on the floor.

Genie shouted, "Three-eighty."

"I got your tree-eighty, little bimbo, and raise it to four-hunnert thou."

Jim's face twisted with disgust. "Why you—"

Genie felt the Inn and her future slipping out of her reach. Her breath came in short puffs. The room began to take on crazy colors and twisted shapes. No. She *had* to have her own kitchen. No more sous chef. No more vindictive bosses with volcanic tempers. No. No. No. She *had* to have it, it was hers, dammit. An insane idea exploded into

Genie's frantic thoughts and out of her lips. She grabbed Jim, pulled his head down to hers and whispered, "I have five-hundred thousand. If you have that, too, we can take this pig."'

His breath on her ear raised the hairs on the back of her neck. "I have half a million. And I like the idea of being your partner."

Pulse racing as if she'd run a hundred meter dash, she grinned and restrained herself from fist pumping.

Jim smiled, straightened up, and said, "Four hundred-ten thousand."

Tony sneered. "Yada, yada, yada. Four-tirty." Genie clutched Jim's warm hand to her cold one.

"Four hundred-fifty thousand."

Tony nearly spat at her. "Five-hunnert thou. Top that, bimbo."

Genie vibrated with rage. "Five fifty."

Disbelief crossed the hairy man's face. He mouthed an obscenity. "Eight hunnert."

Did he really have more cash in hand, than she and Jim could amass?

Heart thundering in her chest, Genie shouted, "Eight-hundred fifty thousand."

The ugly man's face darkened. "Nine-hunnert."

Dear God, this jerk could become owner of *her* Inn. She knew life wasn't fair, but how could such a horrible thing be allowed to happen? She closed her eyes and prayed to Saint Lawrence, Saint Rita *and* Saint Cayetano.

Jim cleared his throat. "One million dollars."

Tony swore a blue streak and stomped out of the Inn. Dick followed close on his heels, babbling apologies and protesting his lack of involvement in the biddings. The silence in the foyer was deafening.

Beth's blonde bobble head swiveled between Jim and Genie.

"Going once? Going twice? *Sold* to the highest bidder."

CHAPTER THREE

Jim sat in Sips Coffee Shop, dipped chocolate biscotti into his espresso, and watched the cookie crumble into his cup. Well, *there* was a metaphor for today's event. *What was he thinking?* Why hadn't he stopped the proceedings, taken Genie outside and talked some sense into her? But, no, just like old times, the adrenaline rush that came with taking crazy risks overtook him—and he gambled big time. He won the property—but now he had to figure out how he would pay for repairs. Where would they get the money for *that*?

Genie put her small hand over his. "A million dollars for your thoughts?"

He gave her a wry grin, pulled the worn medallion out of his pocket and placed it on the table. "I think Saint Aloysius Gonzaga was busy protecting other compulsive gamblers today."

Surprise crossed Genie's face. "I knew you were a big poker player in high school. I had no idea—"

"My parents did a great job of 'helping' me out, covering up for their one and only son, making things right. Bailed me out of jail, paid off debts, and did everything they could to rescue me. They had no idea they were enabling me."

"Are you still—?"

"A compulsive gambler?" He rubbed the scar on his eyebrow. "That all came to a crashing halt about ten years ago. I thought. Until today."

She covered her mouth with both hands. "I'm so sorry. What did I do to you?"

"Not your fault."

"Yes, it is. It was my stupid idea, my poor impulse control. And my saints."

He raised a questioning eyebrow.

"I prayed to the patron saints of chefs, impossible dreams, and gamblers."

"Whoa. Three against one. Hardly fair."

She held up her palms. "I was desperate. I *had* to have the Inn. She was my way out of my nightmare job." She told him about the madman boss and his abusive, controlling behaviors. "When a frying pan nearly hit my head, I threw it back at him. I bolted out of the kitchen. Next thing I knew I was in my car, stopped at red light in Victory Shores. I didn't want to go home, I was too upset, so I drove around. And that's when I saw the Inn with the for sale sign." She sighed. "I wanted it so badly, I wasn't thinking straight. I had no right to drag you into this."

"No, I did it to me. You didn't cause it, you can't cure it and you can't control it. I have a chronic, relapsing disease. Today was a major relapse." *I really need to call my sponsor and find a meeting.*

"But you wanted the Inn, didn't you?" Genie placed a tentative hand on his.

"Yes—but what I did was *crazy*." Jim shook his head. "I spent every dime I had, plus every one *you* had. Now what do we do?"

She let out a long breath. "We do what we're good at. I'm an outstanding chef. You're an experienced hotel manager. We're under forty. We have our health and are *extremely* motivated to succeed. I'd say we have an embarrassment of riches. Partners?" She extended a hand.

A small flame of hope flickered in Jim's mind. He reached out and squeezed her fingers. "Seriously?"

"Yes." She withdrew her hand slowly and sipped her latte. "Why did you want *this* place?"

"The old girl called to me, begged me to save her." He gave Genie a wistful smile. "Do I sound crazy?"

"You call the Inn 'she,' too?"

"Yes, she's like a Grand old dame who's fallen on hard times. Remember the parties? The famous people who stayed and played there? Celebrities came to the Inn because they knew their privacy and secrets were safe with us. If those walls could talk! Every day was new and exciting. I would love to bring back her glory days."

Genie leaped up, ran around the table, and threw her arms around him. "I have the same dream. We *can* do it!"

He hesitated for a moment, then returned the gesture, his hands unable to resist lingering on her luscious curves just a tad too long. Genie's inviting cleavage made him wish they were somewhere private. He could scarcely breathe and had to shake his head to dispel naughty images of nuzzling her soft breasts. "We can do what?"

She sat down again, but clung to his hands. "I've done the research. The Inn should be in the National Park Service Historic Registry—but it isn't. If we can get her added to the Registry, there are laws and standards about how we make the rehabilitation. We can bring it up to modern codes, but have to use certain treatments—"

"I hate to burst your bubble, but where will we get the money to do all this?" He wasn't sure he could afford too many more big gambles like this last one.

Her face flushed and her sapphire blue eyes sparkled. "If we can get her added to the Registry, we'll qualify for special low interest loans. *And* for a major tax credit. *And* we have a million dollars in equity."

"Pretty, smart—and you say you can cook? If you can do all that, you *are* a genie."

She released his hands, pulled her

shoulders back, and inadvertently gave him a better glimpse of her bosom. Genie gave him a scalding look. "Are you *challenging* my cooking, Mr. Rawlings?"

Uh-oh. He never dreamed of the shy little Genie he'd known having a temper. Jim couldn't resist tweaking her. "I'm sure you're a solid cook."

She stood, almost knocking her chair over. "*Solid*? What the hell does that mean? Average? Good enough to make the turkey for Thanksgiving dinner for the family—but not good enough to cook for guests? Tell you what, Mr. Critic, you come to my house for dinner tomorrow night." She scribbled her address on a business card and threw it on the table. "*My* food makes men go *weak* at the knees."

Hypnotized by the sway of her voluptuous ass as she stalked out of the nearly empty café, Jim bet it wasn't just this saucy woman's cooking that made strong men weak.

Tony "the Wolf" Aiolfo sat in his black

Cadillac Seville across from the stupid ass little coffee shop, and drummed his fingers on the steering wheel. It didn't add up. How had those two out-gamed him? He could tell the pair wasn't a *real* couple. Was he supposed to believe that in the blink of an eye the bimbo with the big tits convinced Ichabod Crane to throw in with her? They *had* to be shilling for Head, trying to drive up the price and pick his pockets.

"Cheap and easy," Dick Head had assured him. "My wife's the realtor. You'll get the place for a song. Trust me." Why had he believed a cop? He of all people knew how crooked cops could be.

Tony had been somebody's boy since he was a squat twelve-year old cracking his knuckles and crushing cans and bottles with his bare hands. Hanging on the street corner with his so-called friends, the big boys got their jollies by sending him on impossible missions. Dying to be liked by the older kids, Tony jumped when they said how high. He made it a point of not only accomplishing the tasks, but exceeding their demands.

One day, they all got more than they

bargained for.

"Yo, Monkey Boy," one of the older guys said, cigarette dangling out of the corner of his mouth. "Get me a carton of Luckies."

"I ain't got no money," Tony said. Not to mention the fact that he was clearly underage and the shopkeeper would chase him out with a broomstick.

"Who said you're gonna pay for it?" The other boy sneered. "We'll distract the old guy. You grab a carton and run like hell. Meet us at the playground."

That day, when the boys threw cherry bombs down an aisle, the store owner *was* distracted. What they didn't know was that the old guy had grown tired of the constant harassment by the hoods and had installed a video camera and recorder. Captured on VHS tape for posterity as he grabbed three cartons of cigarettes and looked straight at the camera, Tony's prominent nose, big ears, and thick eyebrows made it easy to identify the thief. The arrest was swift and merciless. Exasperated by their out of control son, Tony's parents had decided he needed to learn a lesson and didn't bail him out of jail for the night. What his mother and father didn't know was the cops thought it would be funny to put the short, ugly boy in with a hardened gang banger twice his age. The next morning, Tony was battered, bloody, and bruised—but alive. The gang banger, on the other hand, did not fare as well with a crushed windpipe.

His parents threatened to sue for endangerment and all charges against Tony melted away. A representative from the local police benevolent society came to his home bearing gifts of food, liquor, and a sizable check. Not only did Tony's standing with the kids in the neighborhood go up, but also with his parents. That week, he learned a little dishonesty went a long way—and later that a lot of corruption would take him even further. *Quid pro quo.* You scratch my back, I scratch yours. Assisted by many a uniform along the way, he'd climbed his way up the ladder of crime.

Being an enforcer for the Newark family had its benefits, but he never would have the kind of respect that his boss, Vinny, had—not until he had his own setup. His boss hadn't liked the idea at first. Thought Tony was going to cut into his profits. But when he heard it was in a different state, Vinny's eyes lit up. New turf, new business opportunities. He gave Tony his blessings, but told him he had to do it on his own, prove he was a *real* family member. Then they'd talk. Just like when he was a kid, he'd been prepared to exceed expectations.

Today, however, he'd been conned out of the one thing he really wanted in life—his very own casino. By what appeared to be a couple of rubes, no less. And it pissed him off. He *really* needed a cigarette right now but that damned cancer scare a few months back had him chewing gum like no tomorrow. He pulled out a pack of Chewy Blewy and crammed three pieces into his mouth, grinding his teeth into the spit covered glob with a venomous crunch.

The coffee shop door flew open and the redhead bolted out like her fat ass was on fire. *Well, well, well.* Was she running to see Dick Head? He put the car in gear and decided to sniff out her trail.

He watched the bimbo jump into her

Toyota Corolla and pull out of the parking place, driving a little too fast for an innocent person.

The woman looked into her rear view mirror and locked gazes with Tony. Her eyes widened and the car veered erratically toward the shoulder, then righted itself.

Inexplicably, the car slowed down to a crawl. He nearly ran up her tailpipe, she was going so slow. *What is she up to?*

Driving five miles below the speed limit, she crept along the main roads, passing an organic grocery store and high-end wine shop. Stuck to her bumper like a magnet, Tony made no effort to pretend he was just sightseeing.

He grinned at her. "Hope yer enjoying the sight of me, sweetie, 'cause I ain't goin' far."

Without warning, she pulled into the police station, began honking her horn and waving frantically at a cop in the parking lot. The cop jogged over to the side of her car and leaned down to talk to the bimbo who turned and pointed at Tony's Cadillac.

Gunning the engine, he took off, tires squealing to high heaven. *The bitch.*

Chomping relentlessly on the gum, Tony sped onto the highway, slowing down only when he saw an upcoming exit for a nearby town. *Unfriggin' believable.* The bimbo *was* in cahoots with Dick Head. First sign of trouble, she ran *straight* to the VSPD.

Clearly, they were gaming him. *But what's the con?* Did they think they could jack the price up so high he'd pay triple what the shit hole was worth? Or did they think he'd come on his knees begging? The only one who belonged on her knees right now was that bitch. He bet she was doing the chief in his office right now, laughing at him, and planning her next move.

Well, he had a few moves of his own. He couldn't touch the Chief of Police—but he could go after that bimbo and teach her a few lessons.

Just like everyone else in his life, she'd learn to fear the Wolf.

CHAPTER FOUR

Jim's sponsor answered on the second ring. In recovery for over thirty years, Brady was always there for him. He knew what this disease was and how it burrowed into a person's brain like an earwig and wouldn't let go. Jim took a deep breath and poured out his story, ending with the thug's plans for converting the Victory Shores Inn into a casino.

"It was like a knife in my heart when he said that, Brady. I couldn't let him get it. I *had* to take the risk—or lose it forever."

"Playing a long-shot, my friend? Or is this really a new career opportunity for you? *You* are the only person who can decide if this falls into the same category as poker and ponies."

Jim sighed. "I'm scared. I have to get out of La Bonne Chance Resort and Casino. I keep walking past the poker rooms and blackjack tables, even when there's no reason for me to be near them. If I stay there much longer, I'm going to fall down that rabbit hole again. When I saw the Inn, I knew it was an opportunity to do what I love—away from temptation."

"I wondered how long it would take you to figure that out," Brady said. "I've been worried about you being back in that environment. So now what?"

"I'm not selling the Inn. I'm staying in Victory Shores. This is an investment in my future."

"I'm hearing some doubt in your voice, Jim. Why don't you go to a meeting? Today. Only *you* can decide if this is your disease talking to you—or if it's the right thing to do."

Jim's heart sank. He was hoping Brady would wave his magic sponsor's wand, tell him the answer to his question, and take away his fears. His brain knew Brady was right, but the little whispers of doubts nagged at him, making him worry that his compulsion might be in charge of his life again. He rubbed the scar on his eyebrow. Not this time. Not while he knew how to get help. "There are no meetings in Victory Shores."

"Hold on," Brady said. "I'll find one for you." A keyboard clicked in the background. "You're in luck. There are three meetings in Rochester. And a bunch in Victory. Not surprised, now the casino is there. Poor suckers. They're like moths to the flame."

"Utica's over three hours away. I'll stick with Rochester and stay away from the casino, at least until I have to go in after the holiday and give them my written notice."

Brady laughed. "Good answer." His sponsor gave him the list of times and addresses. Luckily, one would begin in an hour at Rochester General Hospital. "You need to talk, call me day or night. You know the drill."

"I know, I know. It works if I work it—that's why they're called steps." Jim hit the end button and took a deep breath. If he drove fast, he had just enough time to get there before the meeting started.

A man dressed in a dark suit, blue oxford shirt, and red and white striped tie called the meeting to order promptly at seven-thirty. "Hello everyone, I see we have a full house tonight. Welcome to the RGH Gamblers' Anonymous meeting." He pointed to the sign on the table in front of him. "By way of reminder, please remember: Whom you see here, what you hear here, when you leave here, let it *stay* here."

Jim sat next to a rail-thin woman and wondered if she had more than one addiction. He shook his head. He wasn't supposed to judge others. Whatever her reason to be there, they were both in the fellowship.

The man in the suit continued, "This evening we have a guest speaker." The African American woman to his left smiled. "Let's begin with the Serenity Prayer."

The group stood and chanted, "God grant me the serenity to accept the things I cannot change, the courage to change the things I can, and the wisdom to know the difference."

"Please be seated. Now, we will go around the room and introduce ourselves by first name only. Tell us if this is your first time at GA or your first time at this meeting. I'll begin. Hello, everyone. My name is Eric and I'm addicted to online poker."

The woman to his left said, "My name is Latoya and I'm addicted to playing the numbers."

They went around the room and at last, it was his turn. "Hi, my name is Jim, and I'm addicted to *any* kind of gambling." A wave of knowing laughter broke across the room. "This is not my first GA meeting, but it is my first meeting in Rochester."

A chorus of "Welcome, Jim!" rose in the room.

Then it was time for Latoya to tell her story. "When I was a kid, times were rough and jobs were scarce. My dad ran numbers for the local bookie. We ate better than most other families. I never knew what he did was illegal—until the police came to our house and arrested him." Tears welled up in her eyes. "The bookie got off—but not my dad. My mom worked hard cleaning houses for rich people, but with five kids, she couldn't make ends meet."

As if she was about to get to the meat of things, her fingers toyed with the rim of a Styrofoam cup. "I picked up where Dad left off. I became the numbers runner. I was good at it. Too good. No one ever suspected a little twelve-year old in pigtails with big brown eyes. I asked about how the operation ran. The bookie thought it was cute, taught me about the game, and told me how it was better for poor neighborhoods because people could place small bets."

Latoya shook her head and gave a rueful smile. "A real equal opportunity addiction. I started playing the numbers—and didn't get my wake-up call until the police came for me. I was fourteen, charged with chronic delinquency." She stopped, tears rolled down her face and her chest hitched. "I wound up in a juvenile facility. Those older girls— let's just say, *nobody* should have to go through what I experienced."

The skinny woman next to Jim put her hands over her face and began to sob. He guessed she'd had her share of agony, too.

"After I got out," Latoya continued, "I told my mother I was *never* going back there. I went to church, prayed for strength. The pastor saw me and asked me why I was so sad. When I told him my story, he brought me to my first GA meeting. I knew about AA—but I'd never heard of GA. It's been twenty years since I walked out of that juvie hall hellhole. I ain't never been back."

Jim thought back to his first GA meeting. He'd gone there pleading for help, too. Brady had taken him under his wing, led him through his step-work and was there for Jim during each temptation.

Latoya raised three fingers. "For those of you who think the twelve steps are a lot to learn, think about it in three simple steps: Trust God: that's steps one through three. Clean House: steps four through nine. And Help Others: steps ten through twelve. Thanks for letting me come tonight. And to all of you, keep coming back."

After a hearty round of applause, members of the group shared, one at a time.

Jim knew he was in the right place, at the right time—with the right people. He rubbed the medallion in his pocket and thought about the three steps. He trusted God, he was cleaning house—literally and figuratively, and he was helping others by not allowing the mobster to convert the Inn to a casino. He had taken a risk—but it wasn't the same as his old habits. There were no bookies involved, no ponies, and no poker. This time, *Jim* was in charge of his life—not his addiction. He *was* going to make good on his promises to Genie, himself—and the Victory Shores Inn. After all, didn't the old gal deserve a second chance just like him?

Genie sat in the back row of a Weight Watchers' meeting and listened to the other women share. It felt as if she'd been attending these meetings all her life, instead of just two years. Despite being in the food industry, she hadn't had a weight problem until she hit thirty and her metabolism screeched to a halt. She had added thirty pounds.

None of her expensive medical tests had

Sharon Buchbinder

shown any obvious physical reason for her weight gain—except her high cortisol levels. Associated with long-term stress, her physician told her if she didn't find a way to decrease the numbers, she would continue to struggle with increased abdominal fat and all the risks associated with that, like diabetes, heart disease, and stroke. Considering her boss, it was a wonder she hadn't already succumbed to one of the three. Since she hadn't been able to change her job, she had turned to this support group in desperation.

Of all the people in the world, she thought a CIA-educated chef would have known everything there was to know about nutrition. While she knew about food, what she learned was that she had almost zero understanding about why people—herself included—ate too much. After she'd joined Weight Watchers, the first week's food journal had been an eye-opener. Required to write down not only what she ate but also the time, Genie discovered that she often went too long—almost twelve hours—without eating.

Focused on her job and taking care of other people, she often lost track of time. Then she'd be ravenous and eat so fast, she didn't recognize the satiety signals from her stomach and brain until she was stuffed. The hardest thing she'd had to learn was to set time aside to eat *before* she became crazed with hunger. That meant putting herself and her health first, almost an alien thought until she'd started coming to the meetings.

"Genie, would you like to share?"

Startled out of her reverie, she almost levitated off the folding chair. "I was hoping you wouldn't call on me, Wendy."

The group leader shook her head. "No way. You're our poster child for success. Tell our new members what you did this week."

"Well, I used to try to hide under big chef's jackets and pants." She avoided eye contact with the muumuu clad woman in the chair next to hers. "But this week, I had an important event to attend. So I screwed up my courage, braved the thoughts of store clerks looking down their noses at me, and went clothes shopping for the first time in over a year. I bought a great looking suit and a gorgeous blouse. Now, I *did* have to tug at the waistband a bit, but I *was* able to zip the skirt."

To murmurs of encouragement, warmth rushed up her neck. "Then I ran into someone I knew from high school—and I invited him to my home for dinner. So, this week I learned some men like my curves and just because I'm a big girl, doesn't mean I have to hide my body under a burlap sack."

"Awesome. Next week, we expect full details about that date." Wendy grinned and winked at her. "Would anyone else like to share?"

A sudden, unwelcome thought crept into her mind. Maybe she was just kidding herself. Good looking guys like Jim usually didn't even give her a second look. Why did he? Did Jim *really* like her for her chubby self? Or was he just being nice to her because he wanted the Inn?

If Vinny ever found out Tony had been outbid, the Newark mob boss would ride his underling's ass forever. The family's reputation depended on successful business negotiations. Tony couldn't go back to New Jersey with his tail between his legs. He might as well put a sign on his back that said, "Kick me," because the rest of the guys would never let him live it down. He could just hear them saying, "There's that loser who couldn't even manage to buy a shitty old hotel." No way could he ever let those two idiots—especially the bimbo with the big boobs—get the best of him.

Going around back, away from the road, Tony smashed a window, reached in, and twisted the deadbolt on the kitchen door. Considering the condition of the place, no one would think twice about the shattered glass. Flashlight in hand, he paced the length of the basement of the Inn and checked the old copper pipes one more time. It was easy to spot the weak places and add a little more stress with his trusty hammer. Over time, and with use, the water pressure would widen the cracks. He stuffed a wad of gum into his mouth. Soon the Victory Shores Inn would be his.

CHAPTER FIVE

The next morning, Genie drove past the VSPD and parked next to the grocery store. Even though Officer Webster Bond had been a sweetheart after she pulled into the VSPD's parking lot, honking frantically, she still felt silly.

Web didn't discount her concern, even offered to help her file a report.

But when Tony pulled away, she felt like an idiot. She must have misinterpreted his behavior, that's all. Tony *hadn't* been following her. He just *happened* to be on the same main drag. Victory Shores was a small town, it was inevitable that you'd run into someone you knew—or in this case didn't want to know—on your daily errands. She took a deep breath and tried to focus on something pleasant—like Jim.

He was different from the other men in her

life. The restaurant business demanded so much attention and energy that love, marriage—or just dating—had to come second. This time she had a chance for some sanity. Not that the Inn wouldn't demand every waking moment of her life over the coming year, but it would be hers—and Jim's. She wanted to make a go of it now in more ways than one way. Was it possible to combine work and love?

The dinner she would prepare for him had to be special, sensual—seductive. Her nipples hardened at the thought of pouring warm, sugar-free chocolate sauce all over Jim's body, then licking it all off in slow motion. *Whoa girl.* While she was an advocate of the phrase, "Life is short, eat dessert first," there was something to be said for long, slow foreplay. She shook her head, took a deep breath and headed for the seafood counter.

"Hey, Genie. What are you cooking up tonight?" The elderly fishmonger greeted her with a big grin. Sam always set aside the best for her. Today, however, the lobster tank was empty. That could be a problem.

"Think you can get some lobsters in for me tomorrow?"

"You betcha. How many?"

"No more than two—one-and-a-half pounders."

He quirked an eyebrow at her. "That's it?"

"Oh no, that's just the beginning. A pound of squid, the most tender ones you have. And a half-pound of salmon."

"Ah, that's more like it. Cooking for a big crowd?"

She felt herself blush to the roots of her hair. "No. It's more of an intimate affair—for two."

His grey eyes twinkled as he scrutinized her, then whistled. "You're catering to a *different* kind of party. Anyone I know?"

She thought she'd burn up right there, in front of all the trout and cod staring up at her on their beds of ice. "He grew up here, but moved away a long time ago."

"Well, whoever he is, you tell him for me that he's is one lucky guy to have *you* cooking for him. I'm jealous."

"Oh, Sam, you'll always be the one that got away."

He waved at her as she turned to head for the produce aisle—and ran her cart right into Beth Head's.

"Ohmygawd! Twice in one week. What are the chances of that?"

"In this town? The chances are very good." She eyed Beth's overly surgerized body and wondered how much she'd spent on remodeling her figure. Genie bet she could rehab the entire Inn with the cash the other woman spent on her breasts and face.

"So, are you happy with your purchase? No buyer's regrets?"

"No." Tendrils of suspicion flickered. In high school, Beth never did anything without an ulterior motive. Time one predicts time two. "Why would you ask that?"

"Just wondering. Tony seemed to *really* want that property. Too bad, he didn't have enough cash to seal the deal."

What the hell? "Jim and I bought the Victory Shores Inn fair and square. I would think you'd be *orgasmic* with your fee. What'd you get, Beth? Thirty percent? Easy money for fifteen minute's work."

Beth flushed. "I spent a lot of my own

money marketing and advertising that place. Not to mention organizing the auction."

Something smells fishy and it isn't the cod. "That guy. Tony. He seemed to think he had an in, like he was going to get the place for a song."

"What are you saying?" The blonde practically vibrated with anger. "I did everything by the book."

"Settle down. I didn't say it was you. He just acted like he was used to getting what he wants—and was really pissed off when he didn't."

Mollified, Beth glanced around the nearly empty aisle. She lowered her voice. "I think he's—" She raised her eyebrows and widened her already oversized eyes.

Genie had no idea what she was getting at. "He's what?"

The realtor looked around again and whispered, "From New Jersey." She bobbled her head several times and frowned, as if to emphasize that was one state *not* to be from under *any* circumstances.

Convinced the blonde had been sipping the cooking sherry in aisle three, Genie said,

"Okay. Thanks for the tip. I've got to get going now. See you later." *Much later, as in never again, thank you very much.*

Beth did *not* seem to be in a good state of mind. In fact, her comments were downright bizarre. She and Jim had better get a lawyer to review all the paperwork for the purchase of the Inn just in case. Who knew what the realtor might have slipped into the fine print?

With butterflies dancing the hoochie-koochie in his stomach, Jim stood on the front porch of Genie's house at the appointed hour, clutching a dozen red, white and blue roses, his finger poised to press the doorbell. An American flag flapped next to the door mimicking his wavering knees.

Why was he so nervous? It was just dinner. Right? Visions of Genie's teasing cleavage danced before his eyes. No. He wanted it to be more than dinner. A whole *lot* more. He took a deep breath and leaned on the bell.

Moments later, the object of his desire appeared framed by the doorway, fiery hair pulled up in a ponytail, her luscious breasts covered by a huge black apron that read, *Never Trust a Skinny Chef.*

He handed her the flowers. "Happy Birthday America!"

"A grateful nation thanks you. Come on in." She stepped aside to give him room to pass.

He wanted to grab her in the doorway, drag her into the bedroom and take her right then and there. *Down boy. No need to act like a Neanderthal.* He cleared his throat. "Did you hear the fireworks last night?"

"Yes, some people started celebrating early. Can't even blame the teenagers for the noise. The parents are worse than the kids. What about you? Did you set off any sparklers or bottle rockets?"

"No, I thought we could do that tonight." The words just flew out of his mouth. He tried to recover. "I mean—the incendiary ones—"

Blushing, she laughed and said, "Why Mr. Rawlings, of *course* you meant that." She handed him a glass of champagne. "To celebrate our purchase, I thought we'd begin with a Perrier Jouet. And, since we should be having a cook out—and we are not—we are compromising by having appetizers on the patio."

She led him through the living room under a cuckoo clock made to look like a green-and-red Swiss chalet. "Interesting timepiece you've got there."

"My father gave it to my mother years ago, on their second date." She opened the sliding glass door. "He wanted her to be reminded every hour of the day that he was cuckoo for her. Corny, hunh?"

He clinked her glass. "To corny love."

Genie pointed to the small square white dishes on the glass topped patio table. "Tonight's *amuse-bouche* is salmon tartare on five-spice crisps."

After he sat, she placed a cloth napkin on his lap. The simple motion aroused him. He shifted in his seat, grateful for the camouflage. He turned to the tasty morsels at hand, closed his eyes and crunched into what appeared to be a large wonton crisp—but left hints of clove, peppercorn, cinnamon, fennel, and anise dancing on his tongue. Layered in with these flavors were salmon, wasabi, ginger, and a touch of spicy sushi sauce. He moaned, opened his eyes and saw Genie watching him.

Jim took a sip of champagne. "More please?"

"You may have two more—that's it, or you won't be able to enjoy the rest of the meal."

He savored each bite and realized the chef was not on the patio with him. "Where'd you go?"

"Not to worry." She appeared from another sliding glass door bearing a large platter covered with golden brown rings drizzled with a red sauce and garnished with something green. She placed the dish in front of him. "Sweet-and-spicy calamari, toasted peanuts, and cilantro."

"Can taste buds explode?"

She inclined her head. "We shall see. *Bon appétit*."

"Won't you join me?"

She sank into a chair opposite from him. "Just for a few moments. I have kitchen duty, you know."

"Yes, and I'm grateful."

She smirked. "We'll see how grateful in a while." Was that a signal? Was she coming on to him?

His heart raced and his pants stirred. *Focus on food, dammit.* He reached for the calamari. Spicy sweet-and-sour flavors rioted with combined textures of crunchy light tempura batter and tender squid. He licked his fingers. "Dear God, please serve this in heaven."

When Genie laughed, the smile reached all the way up to her sparkling eyes. "You approve?"

"Mmm. Yes. Why aren't you married?"

She eyed him and took a sip of bubbly. "You first."

"I was." He grabbed another piece of calamari. "To a hot blonde blackjack dealer." He crunched, savoring the flavors.

"And?"

"What happens in Vegas, stays in Vegas."

"Not fair."

"She left me for a higher roller. Your turn."

She popped a piece of calamari into her mouth and ran her tongue around her lips slowly, getting every little crumb. His pants grew tighter. "Sommelier boyfriend became alcoholic."

"Occupational hazard."

She nodded. "I swore off romance for a while. Became best-friends-forevah with every gay guy in New York City. Lots of great shopping stories." She sipped her wine. "Fell like King Kong diving off the Empire State Building for my new executive chef at Asiatique. Man, was he hot." She fanned herself.

A flash of jealousy surprised him. "And?"

"Hot, as in attractive and hot as in temper. As in throwing dishes, pots, anything at hand." Genie shook her head. "He's French—and as explosive as a volcano! I tried to leave the job the day after he threw an iron skillet, missed me, and dented the wall. I picked it up and threw it back at him." She dusted her hands off. "The bastard blackballed me. Made sure I couldn't leave. He threatened every high end restaurant owner in New York State, telling them he'd sue them for stealing his sous chef. No one would touch me with a flame proof oven mitt. My only way out was to start my own business. He's the reason I'm here."

Jim reached over and grabbed her hand. Heat pulsed off her palm. "What's his address? I'll send him a thank-you note."

She stood and gave him a Mona Lisa smile. "Save your thanks for when you're done with dinner."

That was *definitely* a come-on. He admired her lovely derriere as she swayed past him to the kitchen.

As dusk fell, they moved into the dining room. She had placed the roses in a vase and set them on the buffet to the side. The table was set for two with fine china and glassware. Everything sparkled in the candlelight. She held a chair out for Jim, and once again placed a napkin on his lap, this time drawing out the ritual a tad longer. She was *killing* him. She breathed into his ear, sending frissons down his neck. "I hope you like the next course."

Just to have something to hold onto—other than her—he clenched a soup spoon. And a white dish appeared in front of him in the center of which were large chunks of—

"Rich lobster soup with curry." She poured a thick pink liquid around the lumps of shellfish.

Exotic scents rose on the steam grabbing his olfactory lobe, taking his brain to a new plane of existence. "Oh. My. God."

"Some *have* likened my food to a religious experience."

The lobster swam in the smooth soup with a hint of curry while his taste buds danced and sang *hallelujah, hallelujah.* "Any chance I could get this for dessert?"

She took her apron off and sat down. "Not tonight. I have other plans."

The low cut lace top left little to Jim's imagination. Torn between appetites, he wondered if there was an *intermezzo*. He needed to clear his palate—and knew just who he wanted to do it with.

"Are you enjoying your soup?"

"What? Yes. Very much." He tore his gaze away from her breasts.

"Mind if we talk a little business?"

Only if it's monkey business. "Sure." He put his spoon down.

"I think we'd better have a lawyer check out Beth's paperwork."

After she told him about the odd

conversation with the realtor in the grocery store, he raised one eyebrow. "She said he was from New Jersey?"

"Wearing a look on her face that implied he came out of a sewer. Not that I disagree with that assessment."

"I have some experience with that state." Jim rubbed his eyebrow. "Yes, we should get legal counsel. And we need to draw up some partnership papers, too."

"Good idea." She smiled, stood, and brushed her hand along his as she collected his dish. "Ready for your next course?"

She had *no* idea how ready he was.

Genie disappeared into the kitchen, then stuck her head back into the dining room. "Would you pour the wine for our next course, please?"

He lifted the decanter. The nose on the wine was outstanding. What was it? French? Californian?

She returned with two plates and placed them on the table. "Grilled lamb chops, pomegranate-and-saffron basmati rice."

Jim closed his eyes and inhaled the aromas of lamb, the rich red fruit, and scented rice.

Heaven. He was in heaven. "What kind of wine is this?"

"Cabernet—Robert Mondavi Reserve."

He eyed her breasts and sipped his wine. "A perfect pair. Er—pairing."

She covered her mouth with her napkin, but the crinkles around her eyes gave her away.

He savored every bite, gnawing at the bones until it looked as if they'd been dipped in acid. Then he licked his fingers clean. He glanced up and caught her watching him, a smile hovering on her lush red lips. Embarrassed, he wiped his fingers on the napkin. "I couldn't help myself. The best lamb chops I've ever had."

"Think you can handle dessert?"

His groin responded before he could open his mouth. "Depends on what we're having."

"A simple one—hot fudge sundae."

He groaned and his erection demanded to be attended to. He slipped off his chair, onto his knees and clasped his hands together. "Please, please, please, may I have dessert?"

"*Now* do you admit that my cooking makes men weak at the knees?"

He crawled to her chair, reached up and pulled her face down to his then slanted his mouth over hers. "Yes," he breathed. "You were right. You *have* made my knees weak." He pressed his lips against hers and she responded, opening her mouth. She tasted like pomegranates. He wanted more of her flavors. *Now*.

He ran a hand down her neck and found a hardened nub awaiting his touch through the thin lace. Jim lowered his head to her breast and sucked at the cloth, pulling her into his mouth until she moaned. Then he moved to the other breast, but pulled the blouse down, exposing a claret-colored nipple the size of a silver dollar. He licked and sucked at that large, lovely rosebud until she clutched at his hair.

"Stop." She panted. "We still have dessert."

"You're my dessert."

"I'm not too *fat* for you?"

He looked up into her eyes, his tongue longing to return to sucking on that big bud. "Skinny women don't turn me on. I love your curves, your hips, your big beautiful ass, your full, delicious breasts, and your sweet, succulent nipples. I want to explore every inch of your luscious lovely thighs, right up to your—"

She pushed away from him, stood and took his hand. He tried to pull her back but she shook her head, smiled, and dragged him down a hallway. Illuminated only by candles, her bedroom contained a queen-sized bed, large pillows, and red satin sheets. A cooking cart with a chafing dish stood ready to serve.

His pulse kicked up a notch. *This was unexpected.*

She turned to him and smirked. "You should probably get undressed."

As he ripped his shirt and pants off, she released her hair from her ponytail and peeled out of her lace top and slinky pants. She wore no underwear. He swept his gaze over her large breasts, full hips and the red triangle of hair he wanted to sample next. He stood at complete attention, pointing straight at *her*. He reached for Genie, grazed a breast, and she shoved him back onto the bed. "Lie down."

He complied, shivers running up and down

his spine.

Hair draping across her face, she stood over him and drizzled warm chocolate sauce on his chest, belly button, hips, and erection. Then she dropped dollops of whipped cream in swirls along the same pattern.

"Dessert is served. Just so you know, this is *all* homemade." Bending her head over her work, she quickly licked from his neck down to his belly button, and then in a slow, deliberate pace, continued downward. He groaned and grew harder and thicker with each stroke of her tongue.

He grabbed Genie and pulled her onto the bed. "I'm hungry, too."

A dish in each hand, he drew wild patterns with chocolate sauce and whipped cream across her lush curves. After eying his handiwork, he licked his lips. "I think I'll start with these two delicious mounds topped with these bright, red cherries. Then, I'll follow the chocolate trail down to here."

Jim slid a chocolate covered finger into her moist folds, sliding across her center, flicking her until she wriggled and arched her hips upward. He smiled, withdrew his finger and licked it. "Delicious."

Between gritted teeth, she gasped. "Tease."

"Look who's talking. You've been driving me wild all evening." Jim licked his way down the chocolate path. The pool of sweet brown liquid in her navel and below required extra attention to detail, and he lapped up every drop, first licking lazy circles on her soft thighs. She grabbed his head and guided him to her silky triangle. His tongue probed her folds, then flicked at her hard nub until she moaned, screamed his name, and clutched his hair.

"I want you inside me."

He crawled on his elbows, maintaining skin contact with each upward movement. He looked deep into her eyes and slid inside her.

Genie grabbed his buttocks with her strong hands and rose to meet him at every stroke. She urged him onward and guided him, her fingertips alternately dancing between his legs and massaging his glutes: harder, deeper, stronger thrusts. She shuddered, screamed his name, and, he was certain, left ten purple finger prints on his butt.

Jim couldn't hold on any longer. He came with a shout and fell on top of her, panting to catch his breath.

Genie looked him in the eye. "Ready for the cheese course?"

CHAPTER SIX

Genie rolled over and felt something warm, long, and hard next to her. "Oh, baby, is that a baguette in your pocket, or are you just glad to see me."

Jim's eyes fluttered.

"I know you're awake. You can't fool me."

Eyes still closed, he smiled and grabbed her close.

She stiffened. Something smelled—wrong—like a pan was burning on the stove. Had she left something on in the heat of the night? No. She was certain she'd shut everything off.

"Jim—get up. *Now*. I smell smoke." At that very moment, the high-pitched sound of the smoke detector startled them into reality.

He bolted upright, flailing around in the sheets. She raced out of the room toward the smell, and into the kitchen. With the warm weather, she'd left the windows open in the kitchen overnight. Now, bright yellow flames beneath clouds of smoke billowed through the screens.

She grabbed a large fire extinguisher and hosed the window with dry chemical in a desperate attempt to slow the orange monster down. Focused on her failing efforts, she jumped when someone grabbed her arm. "Call nine-one-one. Tell them there's a fire— and it's not a kitchen fire."

"We have to leave." He pulled her out of the smoke filled kitchen and slammed the door. "It's not worth losing your life." Somehow, he'd been able to get out of the sheets and into his jeans, shirt and shoes. He held her robe in her hand. "Put this on."

Thick tendrils of smoke oozed under the door. She coughed, looked up and saw the cuckoo clock. Climbing up on a chair, she attempted to get it off the hook—but was suddenly airborne. Jim threw her over his shoulder and carried her naked, kicking, and screaming out of the house.

Sirens sounded in the distance, coming

closer.

"I have to get the cuckoo clock," she shouted. "It's the only thing I have left from my parents."

He ran out of the house to the opposite side of the street, where an army of wide-eyed neighbors waited in their nightclothes.

A little boy called out, "Mommy, I can see Miss Genie's butt!"

Fire engines screeched onto her street and the cacophony of trucks, radios, and men shouting distracted the crowd.

Genie buried her face in Jim's neck and sobbed. It wasn't bad enough she was losing her house; her dignity was burning up with it. At least they'd had the good sense to shower after their little adventure in chocolate sauce last night. He set her on the ground with care, sliding her down the front of him to spare her a full frontal nudity moment. Wrapping the silk robe around her, he whispered, "You do have a really nice ass."

She caught herself laughing, then realized she bordered on hysterical. She kept her face pressed against Jim's chest, too afraid to watch, to see if the firefighters could save her home. With the exception of the time when she'd worked in New York City, she had lived in the house most of her life, coming back to touch base and reconnect with reality between bad jobs and bad men.

"I've lived in this house most of my life. All my family memories are here."

Her mother taught her to make her first cake in that house. Her father sat with her at the kitchen table every night until she went to college, making sure she did her homework, checking each assignment. Her mother's love infused every meal she made and every flavor she tasted in that house and her father's logic gave her the foundation of a good business sense.

Mom always said, "Each moment is special. Capture the time in your memories, Genie. They won't fade." They hadn't taken a lot of photos, preferring to spend their time and money on Genie's education. So, other than a few holiday snapshots and the rare family portrait taken by insistent friends, the damn clock was the most tangible memento she had of her parents' and their romance.

She heard the neighbors cheer and raised

her head cautiously. "Is it safe for me to look?"

"Yes." He turned her around to face the house. The blaze that had threatened to gobble up the house had been reduced to a few wisps of smoke curling skyward into the early morning sun.

A firefighter crossed the street and strode to Genie's side, his face slick with sooty sweat, his hat under his arm. "This your house?"

She wrapped the robe around her like a cocoon. "Yes."

"I'm Chief Von den Broeck. Could you come with me, please?"

Barefoot, Genie picked her way across the street, attempting to avoid sharp stones and small rocks. They walked around the side of the house, to the back, where the fire had done the most damage. Shards of glass glinted ahead of her. Jim lifted her up as easily as if she was a feather quilt.

She whispered, "You must work out a lot."

"My daily program consists of twenty lifts of any woman who happens to be nearby."

She kissed his neck. "Thank you. For

everything."

He found a safe place and set her down. She turned but her knees buckled at the sight before her and she collapsed to the ground.

Jim knelt down beside her. "Take a couple of deep breaths and let me know when you're ready to stand."

She nodded, then opened her eyes and allowed him to pull her to her feet. The entire side of the house—what was left of it—was now a smoking blur of charred wood. The wall into her kitchen was gone—as were her cabinets, table, and chairs—everything flammable. The sink lay on the floor, the stainless steel charred and twisted from the strength of the fire. Paint had blistered over the sides of the refrigerator, range, and dishwasher.

Chief Von den Broeck pointed at a gas grill pushed up against the base of the home. "The burn patterns point back to the grill." He bent and, using the tip of a pencil, poked at a loose hose fitting on the Propane canister. "There's where the fire started. You must have left the grill on overnight."

"No," Genie swore with an emphatic shake

of her head. "I didn't use the grill last evening. And, I'm a professional chef. I never leave anything on—I check everything twice before I go to bed."

The chief looked from Genie to Jim and back again, his expression skeptical. "Maybe you were distracted last night?"

She flushed, certain she must have turned bright red. Before she could protest, Jim spoke, "The lady said no. And, I was right here, watching her check everything two and three times."

Genie scanned the yard. Her gaze snagged on a pile of silver papers. "Jim. Look over there."

Wading through the wet grass, he squatted down for a closer look, then called out to Von den Broeck. "Chief, could you come here for a minute?"

The chief walked over to Jim's side, obstructing Genie's view. Her pulse quickened and she clenched her fists in the silk robe. "What is it?"

The firefighter pulled out his radio and started speaking in low, urgent tones. When finished, he turned to Jim and Genie. "You both need to get out of here."

"What's going on?" Genie demanded. "What did you find?"

Jim was at her side in two long paces. "Gum wrappers—and a throw-away lighter. We have to leave now. This is a crime scene."

Having chomped through an entire pack of Chewy Blewy, Tony stood in the back of the crowd, eying his handiwork with grim satisfaction. Torching the bimbo's house had given him particular pleasure. Not in a pervy, hard-on kind of way. No, he was a professional, used to getting paid for these sorts of jobs. He knew if he wanted something done right, he had to do it himself. Too bad the bimbo and Ichabod Crane woke up in time to get out. In his expert opinion, the house was a total. Fixing up after fire and smoke damage, combined with the mess made by water, would put a major dent in her savings. All he had to do now was wait for the next auction announcement and he'd get his new casino at a dirt-cheap price.

That'd teach her to mess with the Wolf.

As the neighbors started moving back to their houses, a little boy stopped in front of him and pointed at Tony's hands.

"Mommy, that man has hairy fingers!"

The Wolf snarled at the little puke, turned on his heel, and walked away as fast as he could. Someone should teach that kid some manners. He didn't have time to take care of that today. He shoved another stick of gum in his mouth and tossed the wrapper on the ground.

Jim sat in his car and rubbed Genie's arms, trying to get some color back into her face. Not only had she lost her house and everything in it, but now it was apparent the fire had been set deliberately. "Let's see if the Arson Team will let me into the house, at least to get some clothes for you."

She stared at him, glassy-eyed. "Whatever."

"We need to get you coffee and something

to eat."

Genie didn't respond. She just stared at the house, her face a mask of sorrow.

He squeezed her hand. "I've never lost a house to a fire, but I know about loss. The day the police called me and said my parents were killed by a drunk in a head-on collision, I felt as if the earth had crumbled out from under my feet. I survived that—you will survive this."

He stopped, fearing he'd frighten her off with the rest. She'd had enough shocks for one day. Truth be told, he'd been inconsolable, driven deeper into his compulsive gambling. The day of his parents' funeral, he lost his last five dollars in a slot machine and had to hitch a ride to New York from Atlantic City.

After the funeral, he'd learned he'd inherited his parents' home—but it was mortgaged to the hilt and they owed back taxes on it. The executor—no big surprise—was not Jim, but a lawyer familiar with Jim's habits. At the end of the estate sale, all Jim had left was the Rolex watch his father had put in a safe deposit box. It was the one thing

Jim had never, ever pawned to support his gambling habit.

A pall of grief stricken silence filled the space between them. He sighed, patted Genie's hand, and climbed out of the car. "I'll be back in a little bit."

After Jim explained to them that the home owner had nothing on under her robe, the uniforms guarding the door got permission from the Arson Investigator to let Jim into the house. One of the officers stayed at his side the whole time, watching him pack a suitcase and cataloging what he took. Suspecting he might not have the opportunity to do this again for some time, he stuffed as many clothes as he could into the rolling bag he found in the bedroom closet.

On his way to the front door, he stopped and made one more request. After a lengthy explanation and a heated discussion, the lead investigator rolled his eyes and nodded.

Jim headed back to the car, opened the trunk, and placed the bag inside. Then he opened the passenger side of the vehicle. "I have something for you."

The look on Genie's face when he handed

it to her was thanks enough.

"Cuckoo, cuckoo, cuckoo."

Genie clutched the clock to her breasts and sobbed.

CHAPTER SEVEN

Much to Genie's surprise, when she called the insurance company, the agent who answered the phone had already heard about the fire. Then again, Victory Shores *was* a small town. "I'm so sorry for your loss. We'll have an adjuster out there today. Where can you be reached?"

She held Jim's cell phone to her breast. "Where am I staying?"

"Motel Seven—No. Wait." He snatched the phone out of Genie's hand. "She's staying at the Victory Shores Inn."

After a long silence, the insurance agent said, "Is this some kind of joke? That place is a dump—has been for years."

"Genie and I just bought that 'dump.' When you have some information about the fire, you can find us there or at this number." He ended the call and stuffed the phone in his shirt pocket.

She stared at Jim, her mouth agape. "Are you out of your mind? We can't stay *there*."

He quirked an eyebrow at her—the one with the scar. Why did that make her stomach turn to a quivering bowl of Jell-O?

"The Motel Seven is not a suitable setting for a world-class chef. It has no kitchen, not even a hot plate. You belong with the Grande Dame of Victory Shores." He handed her a pair of jeans and a T-shirt. "Slip into these. We're going to breakfast, then shopping."

The thought of eating made her queasy. "I'm not hungry."

"Well, I am. And you need to eat, like it or not."

As she slid into the jeans under her robe, she glared at him. "Who died and left you in charge of my life?"

He pointed at the smoking house. "Your old life. You have a choice. You can either melt down into a puddle of self-pity—or you can take this as a sign from someone." He pointed upward. "And catch the helicopter ride."

"Helicopter? What the hell are you talking

about?"

He leered at her. "You planning to wear that robe to breakfast?"

She glanced down and found half-exposed breasts. "Crap. Hold it over me so I can put my T-shirt on without giving my little neighbor another show."

He chuckled from the other side of the silk. "At least it wasn't that hairy guy from the auction."

She ripped the robe out of his hands. "You— you—" She grabbed his face and pulled his lips to hers, smothering his amusement with an ardent kiss. She broke it off just as abruptly. "You keep that up and I will have to spank you."

Jim leaned back against the driver's side window and tapped his index finger on his cheek. "Sounds like fun to me." He put the car in gear. "I'm working up an appetite— aren't *you*?"

Avoiding the sight of her lost home, Genie looked straight ahead and swallowed hard over the golf ball lodged in her throat. "Let's go see what my future holds."

Since her driver's license, checks, and credit cards had gone up in smoke, they stopped at the bank after a late brunch at Sips Coffee Shop so Genie could get some cash.

The smiling, gray-haired bank official didn't seem to care that three small children were tearing up deposit slips in the lobby and scribbling on credit applications. He was too focused on the strikingly beautiful, curvaceous woman with long black hair who had come in with them. Genie and Jim might as well have been invisible. After what seemed like a lifetime of shrieking children, the woman left the bank with a thick envelope, her brood trailing behind her.

When the flushed man finally tore his gaze away from the woman he seemed startled at the couple's appearance. Mr. Beasley had known Genie most of her life—he had to be in his mid-sixties. She was amused to discover the man was not dead *yet*.

Beasley cleared his throat noisily. "Ah, Miss King. How may I help you today?"

After a brief description of the morning's disaster and her reason for coming to the bank, the talk turned to financing the renovations at the Victory Shores Inn.

Beasley's expression bordered on that of the subject in Edvard Munch's painting, *The Scream.* "You *bought* that dump?"

Genie glanced at Jim's rigid jaw and put her hand on his arm, hoping to calm him down. "It's not a dump," she said. "It's a fixer-upper."

Jim released a deep breath. "Since we have a million dollars in equity in it, we prefer to call her an investment property."

"Yes, yes, of course." Beasley steepled his fingers. "I'm going to have to see how much credit we can extend you and at what rate. Victory Shores might give you a grant to rehabilitate the property. The Inn is in an historic district, but I don't recall if it's considered historic property. If you can't prove that it's of historic or cultural significance—then you *might* be able to get money on the basis that you'd be creating employment opportunities and investing in the local community."

Genie pressed a fingertip to the blood vessel at her temple that had started to throb shortly after the fire. Where was the aspirin when she needed it? Oh, yeah. In her burned-out kitchen. "I did research online before I had the building inspected. There *are* historic properties on the same street—but the documentation on the Inn isn't clear "

Beasley stood. "Considering this is an emergency situation, I'll add a home equity line for ten thousand dollars to your existing accounts and will speak with the president of the bank regarding a larger loan for renovations. In the meantime, I suggest you pay a visit to the Victory Shores Historical Society. I'm sure they'll be happy to assist you."

Jim led Genie into the Outdoor Gear store and beckoned to a gum-chewing young man in hiking gear wearing an "*Oh Gee. You're Gonna Love Us!*" button. He hoped this kid earned a sales commission because he and Genie were about to make his day— if not his week, or month.

"Yes, sir. How can I help you?"

"We're rehabbing the Victory Shores Inn."

The sales associate's jaw dropped. "Seriously? That place is a dump."

Jim turned to Genie. "Why does *everyone* call it a dump?" He turned back to the kid. "Please do not refer to her in that manner. She is a Grande Dame fallen on hard times. And until such time as we can get her back on her feet, we will be camping there."

Light dawned. "Yes, sir. Should I get a cart or a flatbed truck?"

"Flatbed—we'll probably need two."

Trailed by the associate, Jim held Genie's hand and led her down the camp kitchen aisle. "What about that stove? Two burners enough? Or do you want two stoves with two burners?"

She dug her nails into his palm. "You don't have to do this."

He winced and released her hand. "Yes, I do. I have a chef and I like to eat."

She shook her head and examined the selection of stoves, then settled on one that would do. Pots, pans, dishes, glassware, and a cooler followed. "That ancient refrigerator might be functional—but just in case, we'd better have one."

"Sleeping bags, pillows, blow-up mattress—" Jim glanced at the kid. "—make that a large one, the biggest you have."

Genie gave him a puzzled look. "Expecting company?"

"You."

She punched his arm, but the blush that rose up her neck to her ears was reward enough. Jim pinned her with a serious look. "Think we need a bear vault to protect our food?"

The associate stopped chewing his cud and stared at him.

She smirked. "Only if you're expecting Tony to show up in the middle of the night."

"You never know." An image of the Neanderthal flashed in his mind. He hoped he'd never see him again. His mouth suddenly sour, Jim turned to the young man. "You have any more of that gum?"

Mr. Oh Gee! Flashed the pack of gum at him.

This reminded him of something—but

what? A thought shimmered in his mind, thumbed its nose at him and danced off into the hinterlands of his brain. Jim shook his head.

Getting older is not for the weak.

The cash register tape rolled over the counter and down to the floor. Suitably impressed with his customers' purchases, the gum-snapper told Genie everything would be delivered in two days. That meant at least forty-eight hours in the Spartan confines of Motel Seven. *Better than sleeping in a car.*

As they left the store, she caught herself looking over her shoulder—then realized she was looking for someone. Someone hairy. She shuddered. He was gone. Had to be. She had to get her mind off that sleazoid. "Let's go by the post office so I can tell them to stop delivering mail to my house."

Jim cleared his throat. "Worried a robber will know you're not home?"

She smacked his arm—then laughed in

spite of herself. "Yeah, exactly. They'll never notice the back wall's missing from my kitchen. Or the absence of a roof. The smart ones *always* check the mail first."

He held the car door for her. "Think you can stand being in motel without a kitchen for two days?"

"Does your room have a mini-fridge?"

He nodded. "It does."

"Good. Let's stop by the grocery store, pick up some chocolate sauce and whipped cream. We can have room service."

He leaned down and gave her a quick kiss. "I like the way you think." Jim waited for her in the car.

She ran into the post office, only to find a line queued out into the lobby. Genie wondered if they were giving something away—then realized the Postal Service had announced a price hike on Forever Stamps and people were rushing to stock up at the lower prices.

She searched the lobby desk for a hold mail form, gave up and went up to the front desk, garnering dirty looks along the way. She didn't care. All she needed was the form.

She'd grab one and get out. Genie reached the counter, found the red, white, and blue document, turned around and smacked into something hard.

Envelopes flew into the air, grazed her cheek, and then spilled across the tiles. Genie squatted and scrabbled at the floor, picking up the large white envelopes and looked for the freaking form she'd dropped in the melee. She was *not* having a good day. In fact it was the crappiest day of her life. The only thing that would make it worse was if—

"Ohmygawd!" Beth Head shrieked. "I cannot *believe* what you just did."

There. Now it was worse.

Most of the restless crowd tried to sidestep the scene. An elderly woman leaned on her cane and handed one envelope at a time to Genie—along with a clucking sound of disapproval. A little boy grabbed a handful and ran toward the lobby, screaming, "I won the lottery!" Still on her knees, Genie was unable to pursue him.

Beth shouted, "Come *back* here, young man, or I'll haul your butt into federal court."

All of a sudden, Jim stood over Genie,

holding the giggling child under his arm like a football. "Lose something?"

"My mind. I think I saw it running out the back door." She paused. "I thought you were waiting in the car."

"I was but you were taking so long, I thought there was a problem. Caught this unescorted little guy running out the automatic doors as I was coming in."

The little boy's mother extracted him from Jim's clutches. "Thank you. He's *obsessed* with the lottery."

Jim frowned at the little man. "Stay away from the ponies."

The red-headed child stared up at him. "What ponies?"

His mother dragged him out of the post office as he repeated over and over, "What ponies? What ponies?"

Genie allowed herself to be pulled up to her feet. "My hero. Thanks for grabbing that kid."

"You seem to attract little boys." He waggled his eyebrows. "Big ones, too."

Beth harrumphed. "Excuse me for interrupting you two." She jammed an envelope with a partial footprint into Genie's hand. "Take this. I didn't have an address for you, anyway."

Genie stared at the envelope. "Is this your bill?"

"No, silly." Beth fluffed her hair and adjusted her super-sized breasts. "It's an invitation. Now, if you don't mind, I have to get back to work." The blonde winked at a well-muscled construction worker and sashayed out the door.

Genie tucked the hold mail form into her back pocket and opened the envelope.

Dear Fellow Alumna,

Hard to believe it's been 15 years since we last walked the halls of Victory Shores High. Wouldn't you like to know what's going on with former classmates? The Reunion Committee has worked hard to plan a fabulous, fun-filled three day celebration on the last weekend in June at the historic Victory Shores Inn.

Come for one day or all three—but register early for the VSHS package discount. Bring your spouse or come stag. You won't

believe the surprises waiting for you!
  RSVP to BethandDick@Head.com

Genie read the invitation twice to be sure she'd hadn't misunderstood it. She handed it to Jim without a word. He scanned the paper then looked up at her, his mouth an O of astonishment.

"They must have been damn sure we'd be happy for the business—" Jim said. "—or they were certain the gorilla in a shiny suit was going to win the auction."

"Ohmygawd!" Genie shrieked in a perfect imitation of Beth. "In eleven months we're hosting the biggest party in the Victory Shores Inn since we worked here—and we didn't even *know* it."

CHAPTER EIGHT

Housed in the basement of City Hall, the Victory Shores Historical Society was a large underground warren of filing cabinets and cardboard boxes, all of which were covered with a thick layer of dust. Water oozed from a wall and the smell of mildew hung in the air.

A pale-skinned, elderly woman with a dowager's hump sat at a desk with a nameplate that read, *Miss Harris, Archivist*. She looked up as Jim and Genie approached her desk. "Yes, may I help you?" she asked in a paper-thin voice.

Her gray hair was pulled back in a French twist and vintage cat-eye rhinestone-studded bifocals perched halfway down her nose. Heavily penciled, upward winged eyebrows gave her a surprised look. A sweater hung on her shoulders, clasped with a chain, each ending with a metal cat's head.

Something about her reminded Jim of his grandmother. He wondered if it was the cats. "We need help researching a house—specifically the Victory Shores Inn. I think it should qualify as an historic property." He handed her a copy of the paperwork from the closing. "We're sort of in a hurry." Not to mention the fact that despite their love for desserts, they couldn't stay in the Motel Seven all day, doing nothing. They needed money for this huge restoration—and where better to start than here?

Miss Harris stared at the paper, as if examining it for authenticity, and looked up at him with a piercing gaze. "Well, this is certainly a surprise. No one has asked me about the Inn for, what is it now? A decade, maybe more." She tapped the paper. "Did you check online before coming here?"

He nodded. "The only place the National Register has listed on line is the Westman House. And with all due respect to the New York State Office of Parks, Recreation, and Historic Preservation, the Inn is on the same street, in the same historic district as the

Brown House."

Her eyes widened and a smile creased her wrinkled face. "Well, well, well, you *have* done your homework. Good for you. Allow me to clarify; the house you refer to was built by an architectural firm of *historic* significance. And it's been functioning as a not-for-profit museum. *Your* job will be to prove to the State of New York that your building is historically or culturally significant."

She turned and clicked away at a keyboard. The computer and her desk were the only areas not covered in dust. "Let me see where the architectural archives are. I have an index of all the major collections. Just give me a minute. Ah. Here we are. Come with me." She stood and motioned for them to follow.

Jim and Genie trailed the woman through what seemed like a mile of narrow rows of rusted filing cabinets and mildewed cardboard boxes. He was beginning to wonder how he'd find the way out when Miss Harris stopped and waved her hand over a particular row of filing cabinets. "The files you want begin here in 1800 and go to here in 2000. If you find what you need, we can talk about the next steps. Be cautious when you handle the files. Good luck."

Jim picked the files closest to him; Genie headed for the opposite end of the row. He began pulling out the drawers, looking for anything resembling files on the Inn, which, according to the title search, had gone through several owners and a variety of names.

After a while, and in need of a break, Jim glanced at his watch. Thirty minutes of digging to no avail. He looked at Genie and the intense expression on her dust-streaked face told him *not* to ask how she was doing. He wondered how Miss Harris could work in this hobbit's burrow of mildew and gloom. Jim felt a fresh surge of appreciation for the Inn's tall windows, wide porch, and open vistas.

Genie whooped. "I have it!" She waved a yellowed manila folder. "Schmidt and Stone built it in the early eighteen-thirties in the Federalist style, which judging by the neighborhood, was all the rage at the time."

Miss Harris suddenly appeared at Jim's

elbow.

How had she snuck up on him? *Does she have cat's feet?*

The older woman put her hand out. "Give that to me, please. These materials are irreplaceable." She led the little procession back to her desk.

Jim placed his arm around Genie's shoulders. "Great. We'll take the copies home and start filling out the application with the State of New York."

Miss Harris looked up in surprise. "Oh, heavens, no. First you have to complete a form requesting a copy of these materials— then the Board of the Historical Society will review your request."

Jim frowned. "When does the board meet?"

"Every three months. They just met, so they'll be back together in October." She handed him a pen and a three-page document. "There's also a fifty dollar request fee. Just make your check out to the Victory Shores Historical Society."

Was this woman for real? Jaw locked, teeth gritted against yet one more roadblock,

Jim wondered if maybe this wasn't meant to be. Maybe they should forget about trying to get the historical designation. He had enough on his plate; he didn't need this hassle, too.

Just as he opened his mouth, Genie's viselike grip locked onto his forearm. She smiled, then placed a one hundred dollar bill on the desk. "Is there *any* way you might be able to expedite this for us?"

What the hell was she doing?

Miss Harris stared at the cash, licked her lips—then stuffed the bill into her blouse. "Give me a few minutes."

As her footsteps faded away in the distance, Jim leaned over and whispered, "Where did you learn to bribe people?"

"Tsk, tsk." Genie smirked. "Don't you know you should *always* tip the maitre d' for better service?"

What were the bimbo and Ichabod Crane up to? Tony peeled off another wrapper and stuffed the gum in his mouth. He'd followed them the whole freaking day and still hadn't figured out what their deal was. Breakfast and the bank—that he got. Everyone needed food and cash. The Outdoor Gear store? They went in, stayed forever, but came out empty-handed.

Then, they went into City Hall. Were they filing for a marriage license? Zoning paperwork? He slunk down in his seat and watched the couple stroll past his rental car, completely oblivious to his presence. *Dummies. Why does she have dirt smudged on her cheeks? And what is he smiling about?* After that fire, the two of them should have been pissing their pants. Instead, they both looked as if they hadn't a care in the world.

"La, la, la. *Bimbo*," Tony spat out the last word. "That hotel is mine. You just don't know it yet."

Beth Head stormed into her house, grabbed a bottle from the freezer, and poured herself a tall glass of Russian vodka on the rocks. Just as the first hit of euphoria took over, Dick strolled into the kitchen and cocked an eyebrow at her. "Is it five o'clock somewhere?"

"You should talk. No, *don't*. I ran into the new owners of the Inn at the post office. Literally. Freaking reunion invitations flew everywhere." She took another slug of liquor. "The place was a zoo."

He smiled. "Good. Won't the new owners be surprised when they find out the Victory Shores Inn is hosting the class reunion."

"They know."

His face flushed and his eyes bulged. "How?"

"As usual, you weren't *listening* to me. I said I ran into them at the post office. I gave Genie her invitation."

He was in her face in two steps. "That wasn't the plan."

"Screw your plan."

"I promised Tony I'd make the auction right for him. It was supposed to be his—"

"Why? So you could get your coke free?" His eyes widened.

She poked at his chest with the tip of her enameled index finger. "You still think I'm just a stupid cheerleader—so dumb that she got knocked up in high school and you *had* to marry her." Tears stung her eyes at the memory of the elopement and its aftermath. "I guess the miscarriage right after the wedding was a joke on both of us, huh?"

"That has nothing to do with this."

"It has *everything* to do with how you treat me. I'm an *inconvenience* to you—until there's some sweet real estate deal, you or your sleazy pals want in on. Well, this time, I leveled the playing field and gave them notice."

His face turned crimson and veins popped out on the side of his neck. "They'll *never* get it ready in time. They spent every dime on the auction. They'll go bankrupt and have to put it back up on the auction block."

"Says *who*?"

"Tony!" Spittle flew out of his mouth as Dick shouted. "He'll make sure they don't get any plumbers, electricians, or carpenters to take their jobs. He can delay them for years. Trust me, when he wants something, he gets it. He'll make sure they're buried in debt and *have* to let it go."

Beth slammed the glass down on the counter and turned on her heel. "You better be careful that thug doesn't bury you first."

CHAPTER NINE

Genie lifted a pot of coffee off the two-burner cook stove she had placed on top of the non- functioning range in the kitchen. Camping out in the Victory Shores Inn had *seemed* like a good idea in the beginning of July, especially when autumn came with a long spell of Indian summer to buoy them along.

Holding hands, she and Jim examined every suite and dreamed about how they would renovate them. Matching four-posters, wardrobes, night stands, writing tables, full-length mirrors, and vanities for the huge bathrooms were a must. They spent hours in the Victory Shores Public Library and the Historical Society, browsing books and researching architectural firms. They asked for references and identified construction companies and artisans who could balance the demands of new codes and regulations with preserving the historic nature of a structure.

Thanks to the home equity line Beasley granted her, they'd been able to get the vintage central air conditioning and humongous oil furnace up and running, albeit in a cloud of black smoke and curses from the repairmen. The electric company had reconnected the meter and the water had been turned on. They had a roof over their heads, heat in the rooms they used, having closed off the vents in all but the kitchen and their bedroom to conserve funds. They were putting off getting the plumbing repaired until they had more cash on hand. Hence the sound of the faucet dripping behind her.

Genie knew she was lucky—she had a home and a good man. The saints *had* heard her prayers. She knew she should be grateful, but when December rolled in with a bitter cold snap, it nearly broke her spirit. She still hadn't gotten a definitive answer from the bank about the loan—and the application for historic status was sitting on some bureaucrat's desk in Albany.

Jim came into the kitchen dressed in a down coat, boots, heavy gloves, and a hat that looked like it belonged in Siberia. His breath puffed white fog in the air. "The good news is we don't *need* a refrigerator in this weather."

Warming her hands over the camp stove, Genie didn't have the energy to respond.

"The bad news is," he continued, "things that we don't want frozen have turned into rocks." He rolled an egg toward her on the floor. "Set up the ten pins, I think we can bowl for omelets."

"I hate to be a downer, but this camping stuff is growing old. Cooking on two burners has lost its charm. The air mattress leaks. Every morning, my butt's on the cold hard floor." She sighed. "And, if that isn't bad enough, my bank account is nearly cleaned out, I had to ask the bank to increase the home equity line twice, and the insurance agent isn't returning my calls."

"Hang in there, babe." Jim pulled her into a hug. "I have a feeling things are going to get better very soon."

Just as she opened her mouth to respond,

pitiful caterwauls pierced the cold air.

"That wasn't me," Jim said. "Was it you?"

She walked to the kitchen door and opened it. A rail thin black cat strolled in, sat in front of her, and howled. Genie contemplated the noisy feline. "You chose poorly."

The cat looked at her with large gooseberry green eyes and yodeled. Jim squatted down and petted the creature. "He feels like a bag of bones. Don't we have some tuna in the pantry?"

Genie cast a guilty glance at the cat. "I was saving it for lunch."

He gave her a wide-eyed look. "C'mon. I think I still have five hundred dollars credit left on one of my cards. Let's splurge. Go out to lunch. Feed the puddy tat."

She sighed. "You're right. I was being selfish." Her stomach rumbled. "Let's do brunch. Eggs. Waffles. Maple syrup. Bacon."

"In bed?"

She punched his arm. "*That* will have to wait."

They watched the cat suck up every drop of fish from the open can.

"What shall we name it?"

Jim touched his index finger to his lip. "How about Hoover? He eats like a vacuum cleaner."

"He is a she."

"Oh."

Genie threaded her arm through his. "That cat must have been praying someone would take her in. Why don't we name her Hope?"

Brunch at Sips Coffee Shop was over almost as quickly as it began. One minute her plate was full, the next it was empty. Owner Maggie LaMonica walked by with a pot of coffee and stopped to clear the table.

"Send that back to the kitchen," Genie said with a straight face. "I didn't like it at all."

Maggie lifted the stack of dishes and flatware. "I'll be sure to tell the cook." She stopped and turned. "My short order guy is going on vacation for two weeks. I know you're a CIA-trained chef—and this is *truly* beneath you—but would you consider helping me out for a bit? Just until he gets back?"

Genie bit her lower lip. *Was it that obvious that they were on the brink of financial ruin?*

"Hey. Forget I mentioned it." Maggie turned.

Genie swallowed the huge glob of pride stuck in her throat. "Thank you. Yes, I'd *love* to do that. I miss having a real kitchen."

Maggie almost dropped the dishes. "Seriously?"

"Yes—but only if you allow me to experiment and offer some daily specials that are different from your usual ones."

"It's a deal." Maggie pushed the door into the kitchen and called out, "Earl, you'd better watch out. You may not have a job when you get back."

Jim grinned, reached across the table, and grabbed Genie's hand. "That black cat brought us good luck. We'll eat for free for two weeks."

She allowed herself to enjoy a tiny thrill of excitement. Her *own* kitchen. Not a sous chef. The *executive* chef for Sips Coffee Shop. She closed her eyes and imagined herself in her chef's jacket and pants, whisking up an amazing variety of soups,

Sharon Buchbinder

appetizers, entrees, and desserts—all at reasonable prices.

A woman's voice intruded into her fantasies of butternut squash bisque, goat cheese and leek tart, strawberry crepes, and sweet potato French toast.

"Miss King? Miss Genie King?"

She blinked.

A short brunette with large hips made larger by her down coat stood next to the table, her cheeks bright red from the cold. She sniffed and patted her ski jump nose with a tissue.

The woman's voice sounded familiar. "Do I know you?"

"We've only spoken on the phone. I'm Alyson—with your insurance company?" She pulled her purse off her shoulder and put her hand inside. "I heard you were here and I thought I'd give you the news in person."

Genie braced herself. "That can't be good."

The woman sighed. "In cases of suspicious fires, we are *obligated* to examine all possible causes, including the home owner's potential involvement." Alyson paused and looked

Genie in the eye. "We hired our own arson investigator."

Dear God. Genie hoped they didn't think she set the fire. She and Jim could have died in the blaze. She opened her mouth to protest.

Then the woman put her hand out like a traffic cop. "I know what you're thinking. But it's standard protocol. After extensive research, our arson investigator ruled you out as a suspect."

The wind knocked out of her, her breath whooshed noisily. Genie hadn't even realized she'd been holding it almost the whole time the woman had been talking.

Alyson continued. "I regret to inform you, however, that the adjuster has determined that your house is not salvageable."

Jim squeezed her hand. Hot tears welled up in her eyes and she her lower lip trembled. Deep down, she'd known it, but hearing it put into words ripped the scab from the wound.

"Between the fire, the water damage, and the subsequent temperature drops, it was totaled. Minus the land, the company has decided to pay you the value of your damaged property." She handed Genie an envelope.

"I'm sorry. I wish we could have saved your home."

Genie watched through blurry eyes as the woman left the restaurant. *Dammit. It just wasn't fair. How much was a person supposed to take?*

She withdrew the papers from the envelope, looked down and gasped.

Jim leaped to his feet. "What is it? You look as if you're going to faint."

She handed him the check without a word.

He ran his fingers back and forth across the numbers.

Genie leaped out of her seat and began jumping up and down. "Call the architect! Get Restoration Hardware on the line. We can start the renovations."

Jim grabbed her and swung her around, knocking into empty tables and chairs. He stopped dancing. "There's something we have to do first for our lucky charm."

Breathless, she could barely speak. "What's that?"

"We can buy Hope a *lot* of cat food with five hundred thousand dollars."

Richard Head could scarcely believe his eyes when he read the insurance company's report to the Fire Investigation Team. Not only had Genie King been absolved of any wrong doing, but they paid her a ridiculous amount of money for the house. Who knew the dump was worth that much? Tony Aiolfo had been certain that torching her home would push her over the edge and force her into selling the Inn. He'd even returned to New Jersey to await the call from Beth offering him the place at a fire sale price.

Instead of falling into a pile of manure and drowning, those idiots had come out smelling like the New York State flower—all thanks to the crook's not-so-well-laid plans. Pacing his office, Dick rearranged his high school baseball trophies and straightened framed photographs of himself with various dignitaries.

What was he going to tell Tony the Wolf?

CHAPTER TEN

"Order up," Genie shouted through the serving window.

"I'm coming, I'm coming." Maggie hustled into the kitchen after seating yet another out-of-town couple. "You know, all I wanted was for you to fill in for two weeks. I never expected you to stay on after Earl went AWOL and turn this place into a celebrity food show."

Genie put a hand on her hip. "You mad at me?"

Maggie grinned. "Hell no! We've gotten rave reviews from the local papers, and now I suspect that Mr. and Mrs. Incognito out there just might be food critics for a New York City newspaper."

Jim looked up from chopping vegetables. "Does this mean we can hire another kitchen assistant? This woman is *killing* me."

Genie shook a spatula at him. "Back to work, slacker."

He bowed at the waist and lowered his voice in an imitation of Boris Karloff. "Yes, mistress, as you wish, mistress."

She laughed and turned back to speak to Maggie, only to find Officer Webster Bond in her place, looking serious. "Can we talk?"

"Sure." She motioned Jim over to her side. "Whatever you say to me, he should hear, too."

Web pulled out a notepad and a pen. "I'm on the Fire Investigation Team. It's been three months and we still have some unanswered questions. Both the Fire Department's Arson Investigator and the insurance company agreed that it was an intentional blaze. The cigarette lighter had no prints and the propane tank was expertly set up—so it was someone who had experience." He frowned. "We have the wrappers you found. One of them had a piece of chewed gum in it—but we can't match the DNA to anyone in state or FBI databases. And we can't test everyone who's in Victory Shores to see if we get a match."

Jim grimaced. "Don't you hate it when ethics stand in the way of getting work done?"

Web nodded. "So, our job is to narrow down the suspect pool to the most likely offenders."

Genie tapped her spatula on her palm. "Don't you have a list of convicted arsonists? Couldn't you look at them?"

"We've already started. A large number of them had to be eliminated because they have alibis. Incarcerated or dead firebugs aren't very helpful."

"There's something about the gum wrappers that's been bugging me." Jim shook his head. "It's like it's right in front of me and I can't see it."

"Genie, do you recall the day you pulled into the VSPD and honked your horn at me?" Web asked.

"Yeah. I felt like an idiot for doing that."

"Didn't you say someone was following you?"

She flushed. "My overactive imagination. I thought the guy we outbid for the Inn was tailing me—"

Jim shouted, "That hairy guy, Tony, was chewing gum at the auction! Wads and wads of it, kept throwing the wrappers on the floor. I remember thinking what a pig he was."

"You *really* think he would burn my house down because he lost the auction? He could have killed us."

"I've seen people murdered for their shoes," Web said. "If this guy felt like he'd been screwed out of something he wanted, that's a powerful motivator."

Genie recalled the gleam of hatred she'd seen in her rearview mirror that day. *Yes, that thug is capable of arson—and murder.*

Web looked up from his notes. "Did either of you happen to catch his last name?"

Genie shook her head. "No, but your boss seemed to know him. Kept slapping him on the back and telling him what a great casino it would make."

It was Web's turn to look surprised. "My boss?"

"Yeah. The Chief of Police, Richard Head. He was at the auction the whole time."

Lips tight, Web snapped his notebook closed, gazed off into the distance. At last he spoke, "Thanks. I'll see what I can find out from him—if anything."

It was all Tony Aiolfo could do not to leap through the phone and strangle Head. Stupid sonuvabitch. No wonder they called him Dick Head.

"So. Instead of putting the Inn back up for auction, they're going ahead with renovations?"

"Like I said, Tony, there was nothing I could do. I can always control the outcome of the VSPD investigation—but how the hell was I to know the insurance company would hire their own investigator?" Dick Head's whine had all the charm of a droning buzz saw. "They usually only do that when the property's worth over half a million. Who knew they'd haul in the big guns for a friggin' shack? And now that the reports been filed in a million different places, there's nothing I can—"

Tony shoved three sticks of gum into his mouth. The old adage was true: If you wanted a job done right, you had to do it yourself. "I'll be back next Wednesday. Make your big-titted wife do somethin' useful for a change and find me a place to lay low so I can keep an eye on the Inn."

He heard the cop's sharp intake of breath—but nothing more.

"Glad you unnerstand who's in charge here."

Midnight, exactly one week after Web interviewed them at Sips, Jim shuffled through the kitchen door of the Inn, ass dragging as bad as his feet. The construction crew had swept up the sawdust and debris and left the work site in good condition. Stepping out of his kitchen clogs, he felt something brush his legs. "Hi there, Hope. Are you hungry?"

She stared at him with gleaming eyes. "Meowrp."

"I take it that's a yes." He rummaged in the pantry for a can of pureed turkey and placed it on her dish. She lunged at the wet food and hoovered the plate clean. He ran his hands down her back and sides. "You're putting on a little weight, my dear." Maybe they were overfeeding her.

Genie came in through the back door, hands filled with bags of food she'd prepared for the workmen.

"You're spoiling the guys," he told her. "They'll never work for anyone else after this."

She loaded the bags into the new brushed chrome refrigerator. "Who says loyalty can't be bought?"

"Did you happen to notice that Hope is getting fat?" He pointed at the creature in question, currently licking her paws and grooming her face. "I think we should cut down on her food."

Genie reached over and patted the cat's head, then felt down to Hope's belly. She stood up, a smile wreathing her face. "She's not fat. She's pregnant."

"But she stays inside—"

The woman who still made him weak at the knees, with or without food, gave him an amused look. "She arrived in December—in the middle of that terrible cold snap. It's now the end of January. So, she must have been pregnant when she landed at our door."

"Poor Hope." Jim lifted the cat into his arms. "I hope your baby daddy isn't out catting around on you." She head butted his arm and purred loudly.

"I can't wait to hit our lovely new bed with the *real* mattress," Genie groaned. "I'm beat and I know *you're* exhausted. The lunch crowd will be clamoring at us tomorrow." She yawned and stretched. "Before we go up, we'd better find a cardboard box and put some blankets in it for Hope."

"There's a box in the foyer. It will be just the thing."

Jim set the cat down and flipped on the light switches as he headed toward the lobby, pausing to admire the work that had been completed. The mahogany surface of the registration desk gleamed like a welcome beacon. The floor, too, had been refinished; the windows, once cracked and broken, had been replaced. He knew the crew was moving room by room, repairing and renovating the space in preparation for decorator approved mahogany replica period piece furnishings.

As soon as the insurance check cleared, he placed the order for twenty rooms of identical Hepplewhite furniture and coordinating décor items with one of the top manufacturers in the country. Out of habit, he reached into his pocket and rubbed the medallion in silent thanks to *all* the saints who had helped Genie and him get the old gal back up on her feet.

He searched behind the registration desk for the cardboard box he'd seen earlier that morning, and after some digging around, found it. Whistling a happy tune, he picked it up and heard something rattle inside. *Crap. Had the guys used this for trash already?* He opened the lid.

Inside was a wad of crumpled gum wrappers.

Tony sat back, turned on the TV, and surfed for the porno channel. *Nuthin' like a little footage of naked broads to help a guy relax after a hard day's work.* He snickered. Dat bimbo and Ichabod Crane were gonna have their hands full when they found his latest surprise. Sneaking in while the construction workers shouted to each other upstairs, he'd gone to the basement to inspect his previous efforts. Annoyingly, the pipes were still intact. *The place was built like a brick shithouse.* Swinging a heavy duty wrench, he pounded at the old copper pipes and made sure there were larger cracks in several major joints. Slipping out of the Inn was just as easy as going in. *A good day, about to get better.* He clicked away at the remote—hundreds of channels and nuthin' to watch. He'd told Head's wife to order *all* the cable channels—but each time he clicked on the *Adult Entertainment* icon, a message flashed on the TV screen, informing him he didn't have dat service. In a fury, he hurled the remote control device across the room and decided Mrs. Tits would pay for the hole in the wall. *Stupid bitch.* Now he'd have to find a different way to entertain himself.

CHAPTER ELEVEN

Genie cradled Hope to her chest, rubbing the cat's ears while Jim spoke to Web. "I'm telling you, the work crew sweeps this place clean every day before they leave." Jim nodded at her as he spoke into the cell phone. "They're bonded for life to Genie through her cooking. Yes, we're up. We won't be going to bed anytime soon. See you when you get here. Thanks."

Hope jumped down and slipped through the basement door.

Genie washed her hands and patted them dry. "Is Web on the way?"

"Yeah. He said he'd bring crime techs with him to collect the wrappers."

She shuddered. "I can't believe that creep had the nerve to come into our home. He must have found the key we left for the construction workers or snuck in while they were working on the upstairs rooms." Her eyes suddenly wide, she locked gazes with Jim. "What if he set a fire here, too?"

Though his heart took a major leap into his throat, Jim tried to stay calm. "The crew put the sprinkler system in last week. I'll take a good look around the Inn, go room by room. You stay here, let Web in."

"Jim, I'm afraid. We barely got out with our lives last time—what if—"

He grabbed her, held her tight, and kissed the top of her head. "We're one step ahead of him. I'm sure he didn't think we'd find his trash."

He handed her his cell phone, then lifted one of the kitchen fire extinguishers. *Twenty suites, twenty areas to hide a smoldering flame that could rage out of control.* Trying not to panic, he began the search on the second floor.

Genie clutched the mobile phone and paced back and forth in the kitchen. "Where in the heck is Web with his back up from

VSPD?"

When she heard the front door bell, she almost wept with relief. She raced down the hallway, across the large foyer and threw the door open.

The Neanderthal in a suit stood on the darkened front porch with a gun pointed right at her chest. "Hullo dere, little bimbo. Remember me?"

She wanted to scream for help but her voice froze in her throat.

"Ain't you gonna invite me in?"

Mute, shoulders slumped to hide the phone, she turned away from the door—and hit the recent numbers called list.

"Turn around. There's a good little bimbo. I gotta make sure you ain't packin'."

As he ran a beefy hand under her blouse then down her front and between her legs, she bit back a shudder. Her skin felt as if it was crawling with bugs.

"Turn around to face me."

What should she do with the phone?

Genie pressed the speaker button. "It's for you."

"Victory Shores Police Department, nine-one-one."

She screamed, "Help me, there's a man with a gun—"

Tony backhanded her and the lights went out.

Jim stopped his search of suite 202. Was that Genie? Socks slipping on the polished hardwood, he raced out onto the balcony hallway to peer over the balustrade. Crumpled on the floor was a body, the thug standing over it.

She was down. *Is she alive?* Pulse pounding, his breath coming in short puffs, he patted his pocket. *She had his phone.*

While he watched from above, trying to decide what to do next, the creep pulled her hands over her head and dragged her out of sight across the newly finished floor.

Where are the police? He couldn't just stand there like a statue. He had to do *something.*

Jim wanted to run to her, but was afraid that if he moved too quickly, the crook would hear him and maybe hurt her worse. He dared not take the elevator. *Too noisy*. It took all he had to tiptoe down the hall and test one step at a time, one flight at a time, avoiding squeaking floorboards. By the time he arrived at the first floor, he was dripping in sweat and the fire extinguisher in his hand felt like it weighed a hundred pounds. He stood still and listened hard.

"Stupid little bimbo. Tink you can take this place from Tony the Wolf?"

The thug was in the kitchen. Someone mumbled.

"Don't talk back to me." The distinct sound of a slap shattered the air.

Genie whimpered, then fell silent.

"I'm asking you again. Where's Ichabod Crane?"

"He went to the police department—took your gum wrappers with him."

"So it's just you and me, little bimbo. You and me are gonna party."

"We're on to you." Her voice came out defiant. "Your DNA was all over that gum they found at my house."

"So what? It ain't in no police database.

I'm no dummy." Tony guffawed. "Enough small talk. Lemme see those tits."

Jim slipped around the corner—and froze.

Genie sat in a kitchen chair with her blouse pulled back, arms pinned behind her. The creep's hands were on her breasts. She looked up. Her eyes widened—and Tony wheeled just in time for his chin to meet the butt end of the kitchen extinguisher.

The Neanderthal wobbled—but didn't fall.

Just as Tony pointed his weapon at Jim, Genie lifted her leg in a sweep, connecting with the thug's crotch.

He dropped the gun, went down like a tree, clutched himself and shrieked, "You bitch!"

Jim grabbed the gun and trained it on the creep.

In the distance, the reassuring wail of sirens came ever closer.

"You have the right to remain silent. Anything you say can and will be used against you in a court of law—"

"Stupid pig." Tony smirked the whole time Officer Bond read him his rights. "Your boss will have me out in two heartbeats."

"I called Chief Head on my way over, to see if he wanted to join us." Bond shook his head. "Said he didn't know you. Only met you that one time at the auction. Told me to treat you like any other criminal."

Tony glared at the uniform, not believing his ears. "I'll have your badge."

"I don't think so. You're going to give us a nice DNA sample and we'll tie you to arson and attempted murder—in addition to burglary, and now, attempted rape."

Tony shouted, "Vinny DeCapo will have your *head*."

"Did you say Vinny *DeCapo*?" Standing to the side of the room, the bimbo's boyfriend voiced the question.

"Yeah," Tony snarled. "You heard me right."

The jerk-off boyfriend started laughing.

"What's so funny?"

"Vinny and I are old gambling buddies from Atlantic City. I pulled him out of the ocean one time. He couldn't swim. Almost drowned. He gave me his medallion." He held up what looked like a gold coin. "He told me if I ever needed a favor, to just call him. I think I'll do that right now."

Suddenly Tony wished he was someplace far, far away.

A cat yowled from the basement.

Releasing herself from Jim's arm, Genie straightened up, pulled her blouse together, and wiped the tears off her face. "Kitty, kitty?"

She flipped the light switch and opened the door, expecting to see Hope on the top step. Instead, she heard water rushing in the background. She whirled on Tony who was being led out of the kitchen by Officer Bond. "What did you *do*?"

The creep snickered. "Just a little housewarming present for you and Ichabod Crane."

She ran down the stairs. The sound of a rushing torrent grew stronger. Water covered the bottom step. *Where was Hope?* Tears filled her eyes. That black cat was their good luck charm and Genie loved her. *Where was she?* "Hope? Here kitty, kitty."

"Meowrp?"

Water lapped at the next step—the one she stood on. She yelled up the stairs. "Jim, find the main water cut off."

Footsteps pounded overhead and the gush of the water slowed down to a trickle, then just a drip-drip-drip.

"Hope?"

"Don't go in the water," Jim shouted. "You could be electrocuted."

In the gloom of the dimly lit basement, Genie strained to see beyond the steps. Boxes they had left down there floated on the water, along with newspapers and other trash.

"Kitty, kitty?" Her voice choked. If that creep hurt her cat, she'd—

"Meowrp?"

Genie looked down. Floating in front of her like an improvised ship was Hope's litter pan—captained by the proud new mother with her crew of three black-and-white kittens.

EPILOGUE

The ballroom of the Victory Shores Inn shimmered with candles. The scent of white lilacs, the first of the spring from the English gardens surrounding the property, filled the air. A string quartet played classical music and the crowd chattered happily.

Guests thronged the specialty drink bars in each corner of the room, and bursts of laughter rose above the music from time to time. Students in black trousers, white shirts, and bow ties circulated among the guests offering tiny asparagus wrapped in prosciutto, crab stuffed mushrooms, bite-sized pieces of filet mignon on buttered toast with horseradish sauce, and petite bagels topped with cream cheese and salmon.

Genie smiled at Jim and squeezed his hand. Everything was going well—even Hope and her kittens were thriving. Not that it had been easy over the last five months.

Between dealing with the insurance company—*again*—cleaning up the water damage, fixing the pipes that Tony had damaged, and hauling the sodden trash from the basement, they hardly had time to relax and enjoy the reparations and decorating of the upper floor. At last each suite was completely outfitted in the neoclassical lines of Hepplewhite-style furniture, the best bedding, marble baths, and thick white towels. Hope and her kittens, Faith, Charity, and Love, had inspected each suite and deemed them all perfect.

Maggie LaMonica found a new cook for Sips Coffee Shop—another refugee from New York City and the pressure cooker world of *haute cuisine*. Genie had stayed on at Sips to get the new chef settled in—and to release Jim from his duties as kitchen assistant. He lost no time getting the front desk up and running.

Genie turned back to the crowded

ballroom. She could not believe the turnout. It was beyond her *wildest* expectations. The food critics and journalists had gone over the top with the coverage. When the stories hit the wires about the CIA-trained chef, the Cornell School of Hotel Administration graduate, and their struggles with a low-level New Jersey mobster to return the Victory Shores Inn to her former glory, an anonymous angel set up a crowd-funding page on the Internet. A thought occurred to Genie. "Jim?"

He wrapped his arms around her waist from behind and rested his chin on the crook of her neck. "Yes, my sweet?"

"Don't you think it's odd that the person who set up the online charity page for us donated thirty-thousand dollars? It's exactly three percent of the price we paid for the Inn."

Beth waved at them from the martini bar and favored them with a Cheshire cat grin.

He kissed her ear and frissons rippled down her back. "You think it was Beth?"

She shrugged. "I know, totally out of character, but still…"

"Maybe it's just a coincidence. She's

never been known to be generous—or kind."

"People can change—look at you. From gambler to innkeeper."

"Still a gambler at heart. I took a chance on the old gal—and you, didn't I?" His laughter rumbled through her chest and she elbowed him—but not too hard. "Watch it, buddy. You've got a lot on the line here."

"I'd say we both got lucky."

"Yes, we did."

In addition to the online donations, people sent cards, letters—and checks. With these generous donations, Jim and Genie started the not-for-profit Victory Shores Inn Foundation for the express purpose of providing scholarships to deserving students to attend culinary, hotel management, or landscape design programs. It was the least they could do to pay it forward.

After the bureaucrats in Albany were inundated with e-mails, phone calls, and letters of support from the town citizens for the Victory Shores Inn to be declared an historic property, the pencil pushers *finally* approved the application on the grounds the Inn would be creating employment opportunities as well as investing in the local community.

Despite his protests all the way to jail, Tony, "the Wolf" Aiolfo was never able to make his allegations against Chief Richard Head stick. The Wolf made bail, failed to appear for court—and never was seen again.

Officer Bond had told Jim that when he asked Vinny DeCapo if he knew where the thug was, the head of the New Jersey mob had shrugged, said he had no idea where the arsonist went, and smiled.

Jim leaned over to whisper in her ear, "This will be *excellent* practice for the new staff for the class reunion. Are you ready?"

She took a deep breath and nodded.

He motioned to the musicians to begin the wedding march.

Monica waved, Miss Harris pressed a monogrammed hankie to her mouth—even Dick and Beth beamed at them.

Genie and Jim had bet on a long shot, and now, against all odds, they walked hand-in-hand down the aisle toward the justice of the peace and into their new life with the Victory Shores Inn.

Who Let the Jinni Out of the Bottle...

SharonBuchbinder.com

A word about the author...

After working in health care delivery for years, Sharon Buchbinder became an association executive, a health care researcher, and an academic in higher education. She had it all—a terrific, supportive husband, an amazing son and a wonderful job. But that itch to write (some call it an obsession) kept beckoning her to "come on back" to writing fiction. Thanks to the kindness of family, friends, critique partners, and beta readers, she is published in romance, as well as textbooks. When not teaching or writing, she can be found fishing, walking her dogs, or breaking bread and laughing with family and friends in Baltimore, MD and Punta Gorda, FL.

You can find her at www.sharonbuchbinder.com

Paranormal Romance Guild Winner, Best Mystery/Thriller, 2012
EPIC's eBook Award Finalist, Romantic Suspense, 2014
National Excellence in Romance Fiction Award Finalist, Paranormal, Fantasy, or SciFi, 2017